IN THE SHADE
OF THE
Mango Tree

For Robin & Val

IN THE SHADE OF THE
Mango Tree

Oil, Politics and Murder in the Congo

Exemplars of how to live and dear friends

[signature] 6·16·13

A NOVEL BY
DAVID PORTER

Library of Congress Control Number: 2012908653
ISBN: Hardcover   978-1-4771-0856-7
                    Softcover   978-1-4771-0855-0
                    Ebook   978-1-4771-0857-4

This is a work of fiction. Names, characters, places and incidents either are the
product of the author's imagination or are used fictitiously, and any resemblance
to any actual persons, living or dead, events, or locales is entirely coincidental.

This book was printed in the United States of America.

Cover photo by Bobbie Nystrom. Guinea Bissau ca. 2006. TravelBlog "le_flow"

To order additional copies of this book, contact:
Xlibris Corporation
1-888-795-4274
www.Xlibris.com
Orders@Xlibris.com
114297

For E. Carew Rice III

ACKNOWLEDGMENTS

TO ALL OF those who offered encouragement when none was warranted, I extend my heartfelt gratitude. To my business partner, friend and mentor, the character of Dr. Lake Schmidt: many thanks for the great adventures, your unfailing willingness to return to Africa, and your unwavering belief in our eventual success. To the man who is characterized by Fareid Chamoun, deep gratitude for your friendship, grand vision, and immense presence in all the lives you touch.

To novelist, lawyer, and fellow traveler Scott Graber, who authored *TEN DAYS in BRAZZAVILLE:* thank you for joining the adventure, nudging me into writing fiction, and the sage advice not to take the constructive process of editors personally.

Thanks to fellow pilot, Captain Ken Malcomson, who provided shelter, encouragement, and a hot tub for an ailing back.

Full marks to Cousin Maria Hernandez for all the suggestions, particularly for characteristics of a villain that will evoke revulsion in readers who have any sense of decency.

Unwavering gratitude to my sister, Susan Robinson Craig, for observations, support, and right-on-the-mark older sibling advice about writing. And the same to my brother Dan Porter for reminding me that

I really should be fishing in the Keys with him instead of "making this stuff up." Who knows, he might even read this.

To my mother, Joan A. Porter, thanks for being excited about my book, although I suspect many of the more graphic scenes were skipped. Hopes are that she will leave a copy on the coffee table in spite of the gruesome scenes the author chose to include.

Many thanks to my oldest friends, Steve Raeder and Bob Materazzi, in case they really purchase all those copies they promised.

For the exceptional young men who are my sons, Dylan and Tristan, for motivating me to be the person they think I am . . . would that sometimes I almost get there.

Finally, my deepest thanks and unending love to my editor, barber, chef de cuisine, spouse, inspiration, and best friend, Hartley Hall Porter. *Sine qua non.*

Certain characters and events in this novel based on fact were fictionalized. Where public persons or political figures are mentioned or described, no historic accuracy is intended.

At one small halt in this great sun-baked emptiness, a single tree grew, a mango of modest size but leafy with dense boughs. There was a circle of shade beneath it. Within that circle were thirty people, pressed against one another to keep in the shade, watched by a miserable goat tethered in the sunshine. What looked like a group game was obviously an afternoon routine of survival. As interesting to me as this packed-together mob of villagers around the lone tree was the idea that no one in this hot exposed place had thought to plant more mango trees for the shade they offered. It was simple enough to plant a tree—this mango itself contained a thousand seeds—yet no one had planted one, or if anyone had, the tree had been cut down.

Dark Safari
Paul Theroux

PREFACE

I
T WAS 1992. Across the United States and, for the most part, around the globe, economic and political affairs were in a fairly good place. This wasn't to endure, but that was only to be expected.

Yet there we were: The Soviet Union was fading into a bi-polar memory. The first Gulf War had been rapidly concluded, the victors on the side of virtue, enlightenment and fossil fuel. Bosnia and Hercegovina had seceded from Yugoslavia—in the short view, an apparent modest step toward self-determination.

Peace came to El Salvador with elections following two years later. The largest shopping mall in the United States, the Mall of the Americas, was constructed in Minnesota, covering 78 acres of retail shops including an amusement park. Nicoderm arrived as the first transdermal 'quit smoking' patch.

Congress closed down the House of Representatives' Bank, whose only patrons were congressmen, where 8,000 bad checks were written and covered. (How the bank resolved the $300,000 the Congressmen owed the House restaurant remains unclear.)

And John Gotti was finally convicted of racketeering and murder, largely on the colorful and gruesome testimony of Sammy "The Bull" Gravano. Positive indicators all.

On the potentially more troubling side, the first whisper of AIDS arrived as Mary Fisher gave her famous AIDS speech on August 19, 1992 in Houston, Texas at the Republican National Convention. A U.S.-led invasion of Somalia was launched to stop a countrywide famine caused by civil war and internal warlords. Johnny Carson left the Tonight Show. The long term consequences were initially unappreciated.

Yet, on balance, there was a widely-held spirit of optimism. The spread of democracy with its promise of good, or at least representative governance would soon arise in such far-flung places as Haiti, the Republic of Congo and the Central African Republic. The G-20 economies were poised to surge out of the early '90s' recessional funk, and that promise of prosperity brightened the horizon, even as the remaining 175 national economies in the world stayed firmly entrenched in morbid cycles of frustrated domestic production and confused political vision. Still, even in those economic hinterlands all was relatively calm, and there are pinpoint lights of opportunity and optimism.

Within this hope-filled framework, the government of the former French Congo in Brazzaville was being led, for the first time in its history, by a democratically-elected head of state. Emboldened by the self-assurance which accompanies political victory, the government of this fledgling democracy was seeking to establish, then broaden, economic ties with new and nontraditional trading partners. Innovative programs for the public sector, national economic and foreign policy were beginning to be contemplated, implemented and enforced. This would not be undertaken without considerable risk. As it played out, the stakes were high for the major political personae of the drama.

For our small town players fascinated by the promising developments on the big stage and lured by the exotica of far-off politics and commerce, admission into the theatre could prove more costly than imagined. At least, should they survive, they'd have good stories to tell.

David Porter
James Island, S.C.

CHAPTER ONE

THE AMERICAN IN the crumpled khaki suit read the advisory for a second time and then let it fall in his lap, still clutched in his right hand.

Abidjan, Cote d'Ivoire Mai 1984 _____ "Travelers are frequently detained and questioned by poorly disciplined security forces at numerous official and unofficial roadblocks and border crossings throughout the country. Requests for bribes in such instances are extremely common, and security forces have occasionally injured or killed people who refuse to pay. In the last six months, the Embassy has recorded several instances in which U.S. citizens were detained illegally by government forces."

Lt. Col. John LeMayne, U.S. Army, had handed the State Department Travel Warning to Daniel Quinton as they sat in the white Suburban. "Really doesn't happen that often, Commander. As long as I've been attached to the Embassy here, heard of only two such episodes." LeMayne glanced sideways at Quinton to gauge his reaction.

"Whatever you say, Bwana John," Quinton answered, looking through the windscreen at the fairways of Ivoire Golf Club beyond the wrought iron spiked fence of the American Embassy. LeMayne looked straight ahead. A flash of a grin appeared, but was gone before Quinton could really tell if his goading had landed.

"Actually," LeMayne continued, "we're headed for a village on the north shore of Legune Ebrie, just outside the city. The morning take from Langley suggests armed insurgents have set up a small camp in Bregbo. Far-fetched, I'm thinking, but nice day for a ride, yes? We'll shoot some photos of the village to put up alongside the chatter SIGINT is picking up."

The big white SUV crunched through the gravel of the courtyard, then pulled ponderously through the gates of the Abidjan American Embassy. The official vehicle of the Defense Attaché turned right onto D33, and then onto Blvd. Francois Mitterand. The casual but deliberate pedestrians crossing the road scattered in alarm as the American official's car accelerated with unswerving purpose toward the outskirts of the city. *They gotta love us here*, Quinton thought, as he watched the frightened faces turn angry.

After two or three miles, the road turned to wet dirt, then mud with gravel, then mud with potholes. LeMayne slowed the now red-splattered Suburban, and made what he hoped appeared to Quinton as casual slaloming around the ever-widening craters. When the craters became ditches, the driver reluctantly brought the vehicle to a halt.

"Nice, huh?" LeMayne said looking at the impasse. He rubbed his eye sockets with thumb and forefinger, exhaled slowly, and then said, "Let's try the other way."

LeMayne saw the soldiers with drawn weapons when he looked into the rear view mirror. He jerked his head around so he could see directly through the rear window for a better perspective. *Not good*, he thought.

The first soldier to arrive at the driver's side was dressed in what would barely pass for a uniform. An indistinguishable unit patch was sewn on his left shoulder sleeve. His web belt had a pistol holster attached. It was empty and hadn't held a pistol in months. He grasped an AK-47 in his right hand, the sling wrapped tightly around his right arm; his index finger was banded by an oversized gold ring that he drummed nervously against the fore stock of the AK. His worn pants were so filthy the original color was indeterminable, and a dusty camouflage field cap was pressed onto his head.

Through the passenger window, Quinton faced a younger man, armed only with a revolver. The handgun bobbed up and down as the youth looked around anxiously, uncertain of his exact role in the event. He never made eye contact with Quinton, glancing only occasionally at the soldier with the AK. He was outfitted in a loose pair of black denim jeans, and what may have been a bowling shirt in a previous existence. A field cap, matted to his head in a fashion similar to his detachment commander, was his lone concession to wearing a uniform.

The man with the AK rapped sharply on LeMayne's window with the gun barrel. The hammering of the gunmetal was nearly forceful enough to break the glass, and LeMayne quickly lowered the window to appease the armed man's aggression. The soldier loudly chambered a round, but kept the muzzle pointed skyward. "What is your business here?" he demanded.

LeMayne looked for a rank insignia, saw none, so said, "Sir, I am an official with the American Embassy. We are on routine travel approved by your government, and we have an appointment. In fact, we are late." LeMayne pulled an Embassy photo ID from the center console and held it up for the soldier to inspect. On the way by the gearshift knob, he lightly pulled it into reverse, but held the brakes.

"We are on routine business for *our* government," the soldier countered. "The toll for this road is $1,000." Just then, he saw the white reverse lights illuminate, and jammed the AK muzzle inside the window, pressing it against LeMayne's face, while shouting, "Out of reverse! Now!"

LeMayne screamed at Quinton, "Down!" as he jammed the accelerator to the floor and jerked his left arm up to knock away the AK-47. The soldier, not expecting this kind of resistance, was momentarily shaken, but quickly began firing at the retreating Suburban. As the younger soldier joined the barrage, Quinton braced himself on the dashboard. A round punched through the windscreen and slammed into the back of Quinton's hand, then sliced up his forearm as it deflected and spent its last bit of energy.

Swerving wildly in reverse, the SUV bucked and rattled over the rutted road as LeMayne tried to keep the vehicle from veering into a ditch. Quinton, crouching low, cradled his wounded arm and kept an eye on the soldiers, who continued to fire their weapons. The last round fired before the soldiers took off into the bush bore through the windscreen and buried itself in the neck of Lt. Col. John H. LeMayne.

CHAPTER TWO

THE SUN ROSE slowly over the eastern Mediterranean, climbed majestically into the Atlantic sky, and threw its first lance of Lowcountry morning light through the kitchen window and into Quinton's throbbing head. The table on which his head rested was oaken and hard, and the coffee brewed some time ago sat untouched. Had the sunlight not interrupted, he may have slept there well into the afternoon.

"God Almighty," he said to no one as he picked his face up off the stained wooden surface. On the table lay a copy of the day's *Wall Street Journal*, unopened. Monday, March 9, 1992, it read just above the "What's New" section.

"Telegram for Daniel Quinton," he heard someone call out. A man was ascending the outside staircase to Quinton's apartment, and the voice was familiar. The sound caromed off the walls of the alley, which meandered toward the Beaufort River and unobtrusively joined Bay Street on its north side. A momentary turn of the head southward, and the alley to Quinton's staircase would go entirely unnoticed.

"Jesus, Mary, and Patrick, Lake. A little early, even for you."

"Not at all, Daniel," the voice said. The screen door to the kitchen creaked open. "Going on noon," the man lied, pretending to look at his watch.

Dr. Lake Schmidt, past Dean of the University of Mississippi School of Communications, now retired, irritating morning person, and friend of the downtrodden, pulled up a chair. It scratched across the wooden floor.

"That's really loud, you know."

"I imagine it is for you. God, you look second-hand," Schmidt observed. "Appears you wandered rather deep into the vineyard last night."

"May have." Quinton replied, pushing the Journal across the table toward Schmidt.

"Take a look at that." He tapped the front page, right hand column.

Schmidt pulled out his reading glasses, held the paper and worked his head up and down, first looking through the lenses, then over them. He read a bit, looked up at Quinton, then moistened his finger to hunt for the page where the story continued inside.

"No point in reading the whole piece, Dr. Schmidt, I think the meat is in the opener," Quinton said, rubbing his face with both hands, slowly pulling downward across his eyelids, cheeks, then lower lip, his fingers finally coming to rest interlaced behind his neck. He groaned.

"OK," Schmidt replied, "I recognize the name of the journalist, Ken Wells. He wanders far afield. Writes about some unusual topics, normally rather well . . . Looks like New York has sent him to the Congo."

Schmidt read the headline aloud,

"Roar of Airboats May Someday Rattle Sleepy Congo—Giant Model of a Craft Devised for Florida Frog Hunters Nears Passenger Service."

He continued,

"BRAZZAVILLE, Congo____ If the Congo River becomes an airboat freeway—and it could—you can thank Pierre Eon, Gentle Ben and Reggie Causey."

"And the meat is . . . ?" Schmidt raised an eyebrow, peering at Daniel over his reading glasses.

Quinton unclasped his hands from behind his neck.

"The meat is, those scraggly Frogs and 'Gators—I guess Gentle Ben and Reggie are Floridians—are out there at the edge of nowhere, 'entrepeneurin,' while we sit running a PR campaign to advance Video Poker and writing a newsletter for old gomers from Connecticut who live on Brays' Island Plantation. Mary Magdalene and all the Saints, Lake!"

Schmidt smiled at his friend, and nodded. He was used to Quinton's recurring bouts of enthusiasm, and shared his partner's desire to look for larger game: the big money ticket; the project that would enable not only the payment of travel invoices, but perhaps an office overlooking the river as well. Elephant hunting they called it. Their creditors would call it squaring their accounts.

Since forming Quinton Schmidt Communications International (to "Do Well by Doing Good," Lake would say), the two men had reminisced about the glories of their previous careers, all of which had become grander, more humorous, and more dangerous in the retelling.

And with QSCI's client list consuming a full half-page (double-spaced and in large print) they had ample time to do that.

"Did you ever serve in Africa?" Schmidt asked. He knew Quinton had spent the closing years of his naval career in Special Operations, but the details rarely, if ever, emerged. Not even when Quinton ventured, it seemed now all the more frequently, into Emily's Restaurant to have "just one" glass of brown liquor with his few friends. Usually, it was only Schmidt and Quinton, sitting in the far corner table looking out the window that fronted Port Republic Street. On occasion, one or two aging campaigners who hadn't yet tired of their dozen or so wildly exaggerated tales would join them.

Quinton heard Schmidt's question about Africa, but didn't respond. Inside his head, which was beginning to throb less as the caffeine kicked in, he was sitting in Emily's. Schmidt sat across from him and Molly was there.

Molly Bowen liked serving Quinton and Schmidt. They both were solid tippers, and she was certain Quinton was watching her exaggerated wiggle when she returned to fetch their drink orders.

As he did most nights when he was in the restaurant and she was working, he watched Molly retreat until she turned the corner of the massive mahogany bar. Without taking his eyes off Molly's inflammatory display, he commented to Schmidt, ". . . dress moves like it's a sack of cats on the way to the bridge."

"Indeed. On the way to the bridge," Schmidt muttered, then returned to musings about projects and travel and prospects. He rubbed his temple gently with a forefinger, hoping to massage loose the flow of ideas.

"QSCI, my friend, is capable of improving the human condition here and in the far corners of the globe. Our efforts would not only aid mankind, but

also provide the principals handsome compensation. So handsome," Schmidt continued, "we perhaps should make a show of being mildly embarrassed by the proceeds of our good works."

"Convincingly, but with tasteful modesty; proud but not vain," Quinton added, looking around the bar. He was searching for the loosely fitting silk floral shift Molly filled so provocatively while she floated like a cabaret singer among the tables. It was clearly apparent the warm hum and chatter of the diners and the chink and burble of wine glasses being filled energized Molly. She moved in an easy choreography of service and seduction, delighting in her central role in creating the restaurant's buzz.

Quinton caught a flash of color ducking behind the bar. He ordered another whiskey in hopes Molly would flutter out from behind the mahogany rampart.

"Ah! Nurse Bowen, at last," Quinton said when she arrived at the table. The two exchanged looks, unnoticed by Schmidt, and then Molly asked, "Another infusion? Perhaps I should recheck your vitals . . ."

This brought Schmidt back from his ambling reflections. He looked at Molly, then turned to Quinton and said, "Daniel, let me ask you something."

"Thanks, Molly. Another of the same," hoisting the glass she had just delivered. And another moment passed and lost, Quinton thought. Molly turned slowly and moved toward the bar. As Quinton watched, the cats in the sack continued to struggle against their fate at the bridge.

The scene at Emily's faded into a blur and Quinton reluctantly returned to his apartment kitchen. He rejoined the conversation with Schmidt. "Didn't serve any length of time south of the Mediterranean, but made a stop here and there in West Africa during my previous life. I'm not sure that really qualifies as serving in Africa. Besides, I'm sure it's changed since my brief visits there years ago." Quinton involuntarily rubbed his right hand; the red scar tissue he was lightly fingering started near his wrist and branched up his forearm like a schematic of the London Underground.

Years ago, Schmidt had queried Quinton about the wound in what he thought was a casual way. "Runaway hedge trimmer, Lake," Quinton had responded. "Nippin' little bastard got me pretty good. Why I don't do yard work anymore." To Schmidt, Quinton's still-angry network of scar tissue did not look like the result of a shrubbery event gone wrong, but he had said nothing further.

"Now the Congo . . . that, my friend, has the sound and feel of the Dark Continent," Quinton said. He brought both hands up to his face and gave it another slow massage. When his eyes opened and the blurriness turned into an image of Lake Schmidt, Quinton asked, "Where's this headed, professor?"

"Are you OK, Daniel?" Schmidt asked, looking at the bleary eyes straining to return to focus.

"Top o' my game." Quinton answered Schmidt's inquiry. "Never better. Fire when ready, Gridley."

Schmidt settled back in the bent frame chair in Quinton's kitchen. The aging wood in the seat, designed for a smaller human in an earlier era, squeaked in protest; Quinton winced.

"As I was starting to say last night about possibilities in Africa," Schmidt began, "I have what might be a workable lead." He paused, gauging Quinton's interest and fragile condition. Both appeared at an acceptable level. Schmidt continued, "A former student—a particularly interesting one—has connections to political and economic interests in the region." Schmidt again moistened his fingers, but had no newspaper page to turn. "Fareid Chamoun."

"Fareid?" Quinton took a sip of the cold coffee, puckered, and sat up in his chair, his eyes now fixed on Schmidt.

"Yes, Fareid. He comes from a wealthy Lebanese family, with ties to oil, commerce in the Middle East, and politics in French Equatorial Africa." Schmidt looked at Quinton to see if any of this was sticking, and said, "He was educated at French and Swiss boarding schools, as were many of his wealthy young Lebanese friends."

Schmidt continued, "And he's Christian. Non-practicing as far as I know, but not Muslim." He glanced quickly across the table, then said, "I understand your caution, Daniel what with your experience in Beirut and other places you haven't cared to mention."

Quinton sat expressionless, but maintained a direct gaze at his friend.

"In any event," Schmidt carried on, "Fareid came to the University of Mississippi, took one of my early Government Affairs classes, and we struck up a friendship. Jenna cooked meals for him, and he spent many weekends at the apartment talking about his family and politics."

Lake and his wife, Jenna, had been high school sweethearts, growing up in Evangeline Parish, Louisiana. She was his closest friend and confidant then, and during the doctoral years and subsequent rise through the halls of academia. (Jenna had confided in Quinton that Lake's father had wanted to name him Bayou, but that his mother had a grander vision for her only son, hence "Lake.") Her passing several years ago had affected him deeply, ultimately moving him to an early retirement in his mid-50s. She was a topic about which the two friends seldom spoke. Quinton knew the wound hadn't scabbed over yet, so he left it alone.

"Most holidays and semester breaks," Schmidt reminisced, "Fareid would not return to Lebanon, but would stay with us. Very bright, fluent in English, French and Arabic; he was much more focused than his American classmates. Eager, you would say, to 'get out there among 'em.' Young Fareid stayed tuned in to events that were unfolding not only in Lebanon, but also throughout the region. He seemed to have a keen interest in all the French-speaking colonies.

"Fareid lives in London now, but he didn't arrive there without an interesting and tortuous path through the fog of intrigue that seems to attach itself to all Lebanese expatriates."

Schmidt smiled to himself, then asked, "Remember Walid Hammoud?"

Quinton worked his neck in circles in an effort to make the lingering headache disappear.

"I remember the name, but not a lot beyond his purported wealth. Wasn't there a penthouse flat in New York on 5ᵗʰ overlooking St. Patrick's? And some enormous Onassis-sized yacht? Or, as you might say, 'a vessel of Onassisian proportions'?"

"Not sure I'd say it that way, but yes, the very one. At his peak," Schmidt continued, "he lived the life of most billionaires, only more so."

Schmidt scraped back his chair, stood, and started moving about the kitchen, looking alternately at his partner and the far wall. This, imagined Quinton, was the Dr. Lake Schmidt that a young Fareid Chamoun would have first seen when the professor assumed his place at the lectern. Quinton settled back.

"Now Hammoud came from a family exceptionally well-connected with the Saudi Royals," Lake continued. "His father, Muhammad, was the personal physician to King Abdel Aziz Al Saud."

"Can't get better connected than that," Quinton interrupted. "Know there's a line in there somewhere about family jewels, but it escapes me."

"May I . . . ?" Schmidt said, canting his head and showing his professorial palms.

"Sorry."

Schmidt resumed his pacing. "So here's young Walid, fresh from Victoria college in Alexandria, Egypt, and he and his family decide that not only is there an education to be had in America, there are opportunities. Off to the States he travels, and in succession applies himself to studies at Cal State Chico, Ohio State, and finally, Stanford.

"Hammoud, it seems, is an above average student, but he is mightily bored. He leaves his studies for the world of business. He pursues fame and fortune and, as it turns out, achieves both, the former becoming more notoriety than fame, but the latter, undeniable.

"How does he build this fortune, you might ask," Schmidt continued.

"I might." Quinton got up and moved toward the coffee pot, but kept his eyes on the lecturing Dr. Schmidt.

"Well," Schmidt continued, "he ends up in the murky but highly profitable world of international arms dealing."

Quinton's face visibly brightened. Rearmed with a fresh cup, he returned to his seat in the lecture hall.

"So during what appears to be the peak of his deal-making activities in the '70s, Hammoud is brokering billions of dollars in arms and aircraft sales for the Saudi royal family. He earns hundreds of millions of dollars in fees and commissions.

"Then Hammoud runs afoul of the SEC and is repeatedly involved in disputes with federal prosecutors. Yet he is never convicted of wrongdoing."

Schmidt paused and moved slowly across the kitchen, looking up at the aging bead board ceiling, which looked like it was covered with curdled milk. He raised his index finger, "You see, our Walid is a very clever fellow. He establishes front companies in Switzerland and Lichtenstein to conceal his commissions, all the while maintaining strong ties with some very influential gentlemen in Washington. CIA agents James Critchfield and Kim Roosevelt are counted among his friends and associates. Even Bebe Rebozo . . ."

"Nixon's benefactor and beach buddy?" Quinton asked.

"Again, the very one."

Now Schmidt, with a full head of steam, squared off across the table from his friend, his feet close together. He is outlined by the light coming through the screen door, and bears, with both arms spread horizontal, a striking likeness to Christ the Redeemer overlooking Rio de Janeiro.

"Now here's where it gets interesting, my inquiring colleague." Lake turned left and moved toward the kitchen stove, the sacred image evaporating in the morning sunlight. The wooden floor groaned in futile protest under his feet, and as he reached his destination, Schmidt ran his fingers along the chipped porcelain front edge of the aging appliance. He examined his finger pad, and continued, "Hammoud becomes involved with Emperor Bokasso in the diamond mining business in the short-lived Central African Empire."

"Now that's 'entrepeneurin' at the edge of nowhere!" Quinton said, warming to the story. He moved forward in his chair.

"Oh, yes," Schmidt waved his hand toward the river and beyond, and continued with his account. "As you may or may not know, the empire was formed when President of the Republic Jean-Bedel Bokassa declares himself Emperor Bokasso I on December 4th, 1976. And, as befitting all self-respecting emperors, he spends a quarter of the government's annual income on his coronation."

"As well he should," Quinton observed.

"Indeed," Schmidt said. "So now his Imperial Majesty converts back to Catholicism, institutes an imperial constitution, and has an imperial crest designed. This magnificent artifact, of course, is rendered in full flourish with golden rays, a crown, shields, and other symbols *imperiale*. The scales have fall from the eyes of the citizenry, and they embrace their emperor."

Dr. Schmidt was now in full-throated lecture mode, his voice easily reaching the rear seats in the auditorium. Quinton briefly considered taking notes, but didn't want to disturb the flow.

"Flush with his ascension—it is uncertain whether he crowned himself as did Napoleon—Emperor Bokasso I declares, with conviction, certitude, and righteousness, that the country is now an autocratic monarchy."

"Hmmmm," Quinton mused, "doesn't bode well for the proletariat."

Schmidt nodded, then paused, gathering his thoughts for the big finish, and said, "The Empire was short-lived, and through the intervention of the French, the country was restored to relative normalcy as the Central African Republic in 1979. But not before our friend Walid had salted away an inestimable amount of hard-won commissions and fees, and perhaps a carat or two. By the end of the '70s, was reputed to be the wealthiest man in the world.

"And my point, you ask?," Schmidt queried the lone attendee in the lecture hall. "Let me connect a dot or two . . . As luck and love would have it, my former student, Fareid, marries Walid Hammoud's cousin—her name escapes, but not crucial to the point—and now Fareid is, as you would say, 'inside the wire'."

Quinton nodded slowly, looking at his coffee, which had again turned cold, then back at Lake. "My geography fails, Professor. So the Central African Republic is near . . . ?"

"It shares a border to the south with Congo-Brazzaville, as it is sometimes called. The C.A.R. lies upriver from the capital of the former French Congo, Brazzaville, and it's sister capital just across the river, Kinshasa, the capital of Zaire, formerly the Belgian Congo. Where . . ." he paused, waiting.

". . . stand the terminal ports of the airboat freeway!" exclaimed Quinton, completing the thought.

"Well, yes, I suppose." Schmidt turned to gaze out the screen door over the rooftop of the old Lipsitz department store to the marsh beyond. "But perhaps more intriguing than the nascent airboat flotilla is the connection Fareid has with all three of those countries," he mused.

"Regrettably, he and Walid's cousin have divorced, so he may be outside the wire now, but not before he made some valuable contacts through his association with Hammoud.

"I know he wants to cut his own swath, if nothing else to prove to his mentor and his former brother-in-law that he can succeed in his own right," Schmidt continued. "Moreover, I believe he tires of life in the great city, and yearns to search for a fascinating and rewarding enterprise. Perhaps a career-defining enterprise."

Quinton sat still. "What d'you think will flush him from cover?"

"A proposal to return to French Equatorial Africa," Schmidt said simply.

Quinton and Schmidt looked at each other, then Quinton stood and came around the table to share his friend's view of the marsh. The screens in the kitchen door hadn't been replaced in years and were corroded from the salt air so they distorted the distant view of the Spartina grass, still yellowish green in mid-March.

"When are we going to London?" Quinton asked.

"Let's see, today's Thursday . . ." Schmidt's voice trailed off.

Lake Schmidt moved toward the door and turned to say, "You know that Hammoud's yacht was sold to Donald Trump and became the *Trump Princess*? And it was featured in the James Bond movie, *Never Say Never Again*. Ever see it?"

Quinton walked toward the door. "Never did."

"Never?" Schmidt asked.

"Never."

The screen door opened and Schmidt eased his way through, the door banging shut behind him. He took a few calculated steps, then negotiated his way down the suspect wooden staircase, worked his way through the light morning traffic, and entered the travel agency on the south side of Bay Street.

CHAPTER THREE

AFTER TRUDGING THROUGH the labyrinthine glass-encased corridors of the arrival area of London's Heathrow International Airport, Terminal One, and thence down the long escalator, an arriving traveler is greeted by a choice. The newly disembarked must pause and consider which of two queues to join: one for European Union (EU)/ European Economic Area (EEA)/British and Swiss nationals; the second for All Other Nationalities. Arriving passengers Daniel Quinton and Dr. Lake Schmidt dutifully filed to the right, joining their fellow Others.

Schmidt pursed his lips and raised his head slightly, looking up at the plain, functional architecture and craning his neck in search of directional guidance on the walls beyond the passport inspectors' cubicles. It appeared to Quinton that the professor was sniffing, savoring, and evaluating the moment as much as looking for the next turn.

"What say you, Lake?" Quinton asked. "Do you sense the gateway to Africa?"

"Perhaps we're there, Daniel," he responded. "Much, if not all, depends on my friend Fareid and his interest in collaborating with us in an enterprise in the heart of darkness." Schmidt shuffled forward in the line.

"Promising," Quinton said, "as long as he doesn't end up as a cannibal chieftain, like Mr. Kurtz."

"Indeed. Although remember, Conrad's man started off with solid intentions and noble vision," Schmidt intoned. "He saw his little commercial enterprises as 'beacons on the road towards better things; a center for trade of course, but also for humanizing, improving, instructing'."

"And that," Quinton continued, "was not exactly his view at the end of his tenure, I seem to recall, as he squatted around the fire amid his collection of skulls."

Schmidt smiled, and responded with an acquiescent shrug.

The queue for the lesser breeds was inching slowly forward, with all the fidgeting irascibility and aura of impatience that clings to travelers who have been compressed for hours in a compartment where smokers and non-smokers are separated by a mere seat number.

The passport checkers slowed their pace, as the line grew restless. Each of the uniformed agents had a signature way of preening and sorting desk accessories before waving the next traveler forward, and mercy on the soul of the offending party who ventured forward before the ritual was complete. Quinton and Schmidt watched and waited their turn, each ensuring neither encroached over the scuffed red tape marking fair from foul on the linoleum floor.

Curbside at the departure area of Terminal One, iconic London black taxis lined the ranks in funereal precision. The principals of Quinton Schmidt Communications International awaited assignment to the appropriate cab by the Taxi Master, and when whistled and motioned to board, obediently climbed in while the hackney driver loaded their bags.

The shortish, solidly built driver nodded at the Taxi Master, then said to the pair in the rear seats, "Cadogan Square, is it?" confirming the directions of the Dispatcher. He looked at the pair through his rearview mirror, taking an opportunity to do a quick cross-rake of his few remaining wisps of white hair and furtively check the result of the effort.

"Cadogan Square, Kensington, yes" Schmidt answered. "I am uncertain of the exact address, but the flat is on the west side of the square. I'll recognize it when we get there."

"Very well then, sir."

The taxi pulled away from the curb, and began weaving its way through the milling traffic departing the chutes and chicanes of the airport complex to emerge onto the A30, the Great Southwest Road.

As Cromwell Road segued into Brompton Road, the National Art Library loomed up on the left side of the taxi, the great vaulting entrance doors and Italianate façade imposing itself over Cromwell Gardens and Thurloe Square. The taxi slowed, turned right onto Pont Street and approached Cadogan Square, rimmed with sycamore and elm trees, a block ahead on the right.

As the taxi slowed, a row of elegantly sturdy townhouses came into view. In a tall window on the second story of the building facing the park, a man's silhouette was outlined, lit by the soft light inside the flat. The taxi came to a halt just below the flat where the man looked out over the street. Even from the sidewalk, his commanding presence was evident. He had salt and pepper hair combed straight back from a prominent forehead, and as he made a slight turn to his left the backlighting in the salon outlined his hawk-like nose. It was an imposing profile. One would expect to find such an image stamped on a coin. The man turned back to face the street.

Schmidt waived enthusiastically as he recognized his Lebanese protégé on the other side of the window. Fareid Chamoun, late of Beirut, by way of French Equatorial Africa and the United States, now of Cadogan Square, London, United Kingdom, returned the wave and smiled warmly.

Schmidt had barely stepped through the leaden and heavily braced front door of the flat, when his friend hoisted him into the air. "Welcome, welcome my professor!" Fareid said, embracing Schmidt in a giant bear hug which raised Lake's feet well off the ground. "You have come to London, and you have brought your friend, Commander Daniel Quinton of the United States Navy!

"Fareid Chamoun," he announced, moving toward Schmidt's partner, his arms spread in a gesture of familial greeting.

Quinton stepped forward, smiling as he offered his hand and said, "Very pleased to meet you Fareid, but as Lake may have told you, that's United States Navy, *Retired.*"

Fareid grasped Quinton's hand with his two huge meaty paws and shook vigorously. When Quinton winced, Chamoun eased up, realizing he had been a little aggressive. About the same time, he noticed the wounded arm.

Quinton returned the ferocious grip as best he could as Fareid said, "Well, retired or not, you bring a unique experience to our group. And you are most warmly welcome here, my new friend!"

In spite of himself, Daniel Quinton was struck by Fareid's engaging and powerful aura, much like the description Schmidt used when comparing Fareid to Sadiq al-Mahdi, former prime minister of Sudan: *He was at once imposing and charismatic, an attentive listener and a great talker. He gave the impression of formidable strength, good humor, and a sort of ferocity that most took to be passion.*

Fareid looked at you openly and fiercely with ice-blue eyes, very unsettling for the newly introduced. Quinton had not expected this when told he was to meet a Lebanese diplomat and businessman. *A Middle Easterner with tentacles in Africa, raised in the scheming, twisting world of international oil and arms dealing, should appear much more sinister, shiftier, and, well, just different,* Quinton thought.

Yet Quinton found himself gradually drawn into the energy and excitement stirred by the engaging up-sized Lebanese expatriate. Meeting Fareid was like walking into a café in Morocco run by ex-Air America pilots: smokey, conspiratorial, ripe with imminent danger and a promise of riches, more intoxicating for the prospect of the former than a remote chance of the latter. But this was exactly what the Americans had spoken of in Beaufort, Quinton reminded himself. It was entrepeneurin' at the edge. The hunt for elephants. Here was a portal through which they could be, as Huck Finn said, "Strikin' out for the Territories!"

"I plan for you to meet Thomas Kanza, my dear Professor Schmidt and my new friend Daniel," Fareid said, lighting a Marlboro and ushering the two men into the front salon where earlier he had been looking out over Cadogan Square. He offered each a cigarette from the opened pack, and apologized (as he always would) for lighting up again. Quinton and Schmidt politely declined.

Fareid began, "Thomas has lived in London for years. He arrived in the U.K. after the tumultuous period following Congolese independence." Fareid drew on his cigarette, and blew the smoke politely to the side.

"As you know, my professor, I speak of Zaire, the former Belgian Congo. Now Thomas, who was but in his twenties, was a trusted adviser and confidant to Patrice Lumumba, the first Prime Minister of the new sovereign state." Fareid continued, "This is not unusual in Africa, as the average life expectancy is so short that many diplomats are very young.

"At the age of 27, Thomas was a Minister in Lumumba's government and was appointed Congo's first Ambassador to the United Nations. He was destined for greatness."

Quinton fought to remember his hopes, dreams and desires at that youthful age, and as best he could recall they included many things, but greatness was not among them. He looked at Schmidt, who picked up for Fareid:

"And when Lumumba was assassinated, the Belgians and/or the CIA (those specifically involved remain shrouded in obscurity) had staved off what they perceived was a dire threat to the Free World. Lumumba was known to have had close ties with Moscow, and was seen as a rabid Communist.

"Worse yet," Schmidt carried on, "Lumumba was a charismatic leader who had captured the world's attention with his audacity and eloquence. What political havoc this young firebrand would ignite among the newly-independent African countries, while the ideologies they might embrace caused great consternation in Washington."

Quinton remembered the turmoil of the time—the early '60s. America was coming to grips with racial integration at home and the threat of Communist influence on decolonization abroad. CIA Director Allen Dulles was concerned to such an extent that he had written "... *if*

[Lumumba] continues to hold high office, the inevitable result will [have] disastrous consequences . . . for the interests of the free world generally. Consequently, we conclude that his removal must be an urgent and prime objective." The politically sensitive term, "regime change" was decades away.

"So after Lumumba was removed in a military coup, brutally beaten, then finally executed in 1961," Fareid picked up the line from Schmidt, "Thomas found his way to England, where he entered Oxford. He was a gifted student, and eventually ended up lecturing at the great university."

"His work on African independence, particularly his focus on the former Belgian Congo, was much admired," Schmidt added. "Thomas's *Africa Must Change: An African Manifesto* published in 1979 is considered a seminal work on the emerging continent."

"This is one of his papers, also widely recognized by scholars (and African politicians, I might add)," Fareid said, handing a sheaf of papers to Quinton. "See what you think of his outlook, my friend."

The papers were of old lightweight parchment, and a meticulous hand on a ribbon typewriter neatly produced the text. Quinton noticed the letters had impacted the paper with such force that the keystroke had pushed some of the characters partially through the paper. The writer had clearly crafted the work with passion, perhaps even anger. The title was "Prison, Exile or Death." These, according to the author, were the three (and only) options open to African heads of state after a period of rule, no matter how long or how abbreviated.

Quinton passed the packet to Schmidt, who nodded in appreciation, and said, "The title sounds so final, does it not? Yet there is another option which appears to be exercised on occasion." Schmidt moistened his finger and began turning the pages of Kanza's treatise in his signature academic style. "And that is what occurs in between time; in between assumption of national leadership, and one of the three endings. Specifically, Return to Power is an outcome; an option possible after all but one of these final options."

"A fourth option, I suppose one could call it." Quinton said.

"One could," Schmidt replied, placing the papers on the coffee table.

Fareid smiled and eased himself back into the heavy cushions of the decorative silk-covered sofa. He looked with pleasure at his guests and reached, apologetically, for another cigarette.

The smell of freshly pulverized coffee beans was complemented by the whirring of the grinding machine, along with the vibrant singing of the grinder herself, Fareid's house help, Nawala. The words were indistinguishable, but the melody was haunting and erotic, and filled the kitchen at the rear of the flat. As she sang, Nawala fussed with the coffee machine and then wiped the porcelain subway tiles of the backsplash with a colorful dishtowel. The rag was limp with experience and warm water, and now flew around the enclosed space with a dash here and a swipe there. She was filled with self-enjoyment; the concert was proceeding wonderfully, just as she had practiced and performed so many times in her head. While she orchestrated the production, the two American partners sat in the salon, enjoying the morning's sensory onslaught and relishing the tantalizing prospect of Nawala's imminent offering.

Today they were to meet Thomas Kanza. The coffee demitasses were removed by the still-humming Nawala, and the anticipation of meeting, and perhaps advising, so prominent an African figure had Quinton pacing in front of the high windows. Schmidt sat in the salon collecting his thoughts, pulling elements of past electoral campaigns into the present and trying to wicker them into a cohesive plan. They were not fitting together yet.

Sun shafts passed high on the windows and slanted down to the Tabriz carpet in the salon, creating smoky, intricate dust-swirled diagonals. Quinton's head brightened, then darkened, as he moved from sunlight to shadow, purposefully crossing the salon from side to side. He heard the footfalls on the marble entranceway first, and moved toward the center of the room, motioning to Schmidt with a perfunctory sideways nod toward the front door.

Fareid's voice preceded the two men who were ascending the polished wooden steps that joined the short hallway into the salon. "Gentlemen! Gentlemen!" he called into the flat. "Thomas is with me!" Fareid loomed into the space, which immediately felt smaller to the waiting Quinton and Schmidt.

Alongside Fareid stood Mr. Thomas Kanza, hands clasped modestly in front of his impeccably tailored suit. With much care, the aging blue pinstripe had survived long years, interminable meetings, and many administrations. The shirt was starched white, and from its fit, clearly turned out after many measurings and fussings on Jermyn Street, the district in London renowned for tailored shirts. *Emmett, or perhaps Turnbull and Asser,* Quinton wagered to himself. The tie was silk, conservatively striped, and snugged with precision into the throat of the collar. Here, too, at the shirt's edges were signs the visit to the tailor had been many seasons past.

"Thomas, if you will allow me," Fareid said. Kanza turned slightly toward his host and bowed imperceptibly, tacitly granting

Fareid permission to proceed. He then turned back to face the two Americans.

"Thomas, these are my two American associates, Dr. Lake Schmidt, and Cdr. Daniel Quinton." Fareid said proudly. Then, "Dr. Schmidt my professor, and my new friend Daniel Quinton, may I introduce you to Mr. Thomas Kanza, the next Foreign Minister of Zaire."

"Premature, my dear friend, premature," Kanza smiled at Fareid's promotional fervor, wagging his forefinger side to side as he spoke for the first time. The men moved into the adjoining room, each insisting the others should proceed first. Schmidt relented and entered ahead of the rest.

Kanza began slowly, measuring the reactions of the group now seated and gathered about him in the salon. As Thomas spoke, Quinton was mesmerized by the melodic, resonating voice recounting the early days of the former Belgian Congo's newly independent government. It was difficult to follow the story line, as it became secondary to Kanza's captivating, musical delivery. Quinton had heard it said people would listen enraptured to James Earl Jones were he merely to read from the New York phone book. Kanza was Jones's rival in that regard, but the message was more sombre.

"Lumumba's fierce anti-colonialism was most unnerving to Brussels," Kanza said, settling into a high wingback chair. Although he unbuttoned his suit coat, and slumped slightly into the leather folds of the accommodating chair, his eyes remained fierce and bright; he looked slowly from one listener to the next.

"After Lumumba was arrested by Congolese authorities during the military coup in December, 1960, the Belgians had their chance." Kanza paused, remembering. "Officials in Brussels engineered his transfer to Katanga province, which was still under Belgian control after independence. Belgium's African Affairs Minister, Harold d'Aspremont Lynden, personally ordered that Lumumba be sent to Katanga knowing as everyone did, that this was a death sentence."

Kanza looked at Fareid, and asked "Will you please have Nawalla bring water?"

"Of course, my friend. I will have coffee brought as well," and Fareid left the room.

"Please continue, Mr. Kanza," Quinton said, looking at Schmidt who nodded in concurrence.

"I shall, Daniel, but please, it is 'Thomas'."

Kanza now sat with hands clasped in his lap, waiting for the water before continuing his account. Nawalla shuffled hurriedly into the room with an opened bottle of Pellegrino, poured a glass for him, and set the bottle down near the chair.

"When Lumumba arrived in Katanga, he was bleeding from a severe beating. Later that evening Patrice Lumumba, my friend and mentor, was killed by a firing squad commanded by a Belgian officer." Kanza gathered himself, took a sip of the water that had been handed him, and continued. "A week earlier, he had written to his wife, 'I prefer to die with my head unbowed, my faith unshakeable, and with profound trust in the destiny of my country.'" There now was a thick silence that hung in the salon, and the room's earlier cheer from bright shafts of sunlight had given way to a room that was scarcely lit by the graying skies over the park. "Lumumba was 35," Kanza finished quietly.

"The next step, I imagine, was to destroy the evidence," Quinton offered, uncomfortable with the silence.

"The next step, yes, of course," Kanza resumed, straightening in his chair. Now, for Kanza, the story was just reportage.

"And four days later, Belgian Police Commissioner Gerard Soete and his brother cut up the body with a hacksaw and dissolved it in sulfuric acid. Decades later, during an interview on Belgian TV, Soete would display a bullet and two teeth he claimed to have saved from Lumumba's body.

"What remains unclear, even after the U.S. Senate assassination investigations 14 years afterward, was the extent to which the CIA was involved," Kanza said. "No proof was found, but suspicions lingered. Reportedly, then-CIA Station Chief Lawrence Devlin had been kept fully informed of the operation by the Belgians, but to this day denies any involvement in the murder.

"In any case," Kanza sighed heavily, now reaching for the small cup of coffee Nawalla had quietly placed at each side table, "Lumumba's death served a purpose: it bolstered the shaky regime of a formerly obscure colonel named Joseph Mobutu. During his three-decade rule, Mobutu would run my country, laden with natural resources, into the depths of poverty.

"And here we find ourselves, with Mobutu severely weakened, forced by his neighboring countries to consider multi-party elections, and he is cornered," Kanza said. "And also here in London, 30 years on, one of Lumumba's colleagues, an academic expatriate, a Congolese fighter stands before his new friends," Kanza concluded, his arms slightly raised, palms opened toward the group in the salon.

Schmidt had been taking all this in without comment. "Thomas, our group," Schmidt looked first at Quinton then at Fareid, "would be honored to assist in returning you to Zaire in some meaningful role of leadership."

Kanza sat down quietly, folded his hands again, and waited for Schmidt to continue.

"In order for us to do this, to plan our campaign and be successful at the end of the day, we must learn much about the electoral context in Kinshasa. Regrettably, for the moment at least, about this we are woefully uninformed" Schmidt said.

Kanza nodded, then asked, "Where shall we begin?"

Schmidt stood, and moved around the back of the sofa. His reading glasses came out of his shirt pocket, but they became a device to twirl rather than to improve his vision. He began to pace the room.

"Let me just list some issues off the top of my head; you don't have to answer now, just consider." Schmidt continued, "One, what sort of name recognition do you have at the grassroots level? Two, do you have any major political party affiliation? Three, are you in any way associated with Mobutu, or is there a perception you are in the Mobutu camp? Four," Schmidt stopped behind the sofa, "do you feel your prolonged absence from the country may be to your detriment? That is, will you be perceived as an outsider, an observer not a participant, coming late to the game?"

"All good questions, professor," Kanza answered. "And if you will allow me, over the next few days I will work to provide your group with a written analysis of the political situation, my personal evaluation of how I am perceived, and finally, how we might go forward together."

Schmidt nodded in agreement, looking at both Fareid and Quinton for assurance. Fareid stood up and faced the group, turning toward Kanza. The room again became smaller. He was now the broker, and spoke with directness and precision:

"Thomas, I will not presume to know your financial circumstances, but our fees are substantial," he said. Quinton and Schmidt exchanged glances. "Our basis will be an annual retainer, to be determined by the scope of the project. We will reach an agreement by the end of the week," Fareid said, "but you have an advantage in the negotiations."

The two Americans were now watching Kanza and Chamoun intently, both of them wondering with Kanza where this was headed. The partnership of Quinton, Fareid and Schmidt had only been implied, never formally discussed. Compensation had been a distant and amorphous aspiration at best. Quinton and Schmidt were now acutely aware of the significance of the moment, and both men leaned forward.

"Your advantage, Thomas, is that you have a strong connection to President Bissoula, across the river in Brazzaville," Fareid continued. "And that has currency with our group. We seek, as my professor is fond of saying, 'To Do Well by Doing Good'." There are commercial interests in America seeking new and emerging markets, and this region has caught the eye of the aggressive investor." Fareid paused, and moved to the center of the room.

"We would like a formal introduction to his Excellency, and you, promoting our group with all your persuasive powers," Fareid moved gracefully onto the sofa next to Thomas. He softly placed his right hand on Kanza's arm. "The entire retainer will not be squared, but a reasonable portion will. Your introduction of our group to Bissoula will allow us to undertake the first stages of your project."

Kanza looked first at Fareid, then at Schmidt and Quinton, and smiling, returned to Fareid, "This is the Fareid Chamoun I remember from the Hammoud days."

Fareid acknowledged with a slight bow, then asked, "Is this not a fair arrangement? One where all parties might prosper?"

"Quite so, God willing," Kanza replied. He stood, as did Fareid, and moved toward the shaft of sunlight that had now returned. In the center of the salon, standing in the waning daylight, they clasped one another's arms. It seemed to Quinton as if he and Schmidt had now become supernumeraries in the unfolding interaction, unseen and indistinguishable, as if they were merely patterns in the furniture upholstery.

"At some point," Fareid, still holding Kanza's arm, began in a softer and lower voice which only the two could hear, "for Congo-Brazzaville and Bissoula, we must consider an opportunity for funding support from Occidental Petroleum." Fareid paused, then added, "The ELF Aquitaine Oil empire cannot dominate without end."

Thomas Kanza's reaction was immediate. He stepped back slightly from Fareid, his features now in shadow, and said, "Be very, very careful my friend. In such business as you mention, a bullet may find you."

"So, Lake," Quinton asked his friend after Kanza and Chamoun had left the flat, "has a new partner just voted himself into our corporation? Or are we embracing a silent partner? Honestly, I think our opportunities have greatly expanded with Fareid in the mix. Just think we need to be careful how we lash this together."

"I agree, Daniel," Schmidt said. "Were he to join us formally, we would have to change QSCI to an 'S' Corp. to allow for a foreign partner. But I believe Fareid much prefers to stay and work in the shadows."

"I would imagine so, Lake, given his skill sets. So, then we would trust Fareid to share information, and more importantly, compensation on a handshake?" Quinton asked. "You have that level of confidence in him?"

"Yes, as you say. But unlike you and me, my intrepid American partner, the Foreign Corruption Act does not restrict Fareid. He may operate in ways that have proven successful in the bartering countries time and again over the centuries."

"Ways of which we would wholly disapprove, of course," Quinton said. "If we were aware they were being used."

"And vigorously oppose," Professor Schmidt added. "Were we aware . . ."

CHAPTER FOUR

O N THE RETURN trip from London, Quinton and Schmidt were wedged aboard American Flight 101 in middle seats in common carriage class, herded through the international terminal at JFK, Yellow Cabbed cross town to LaGuardia, and finally, turbo-propped to Charleston, SC.

They found themselves driving to Beaufort from the Charleston Regional Airport in a gathering rainsquall. Travel was taking its toll on the partners. The trip home had been mostly a contemplative time, Quinton lost in thoughts of returning to a region that still held haunting images; Schmidt filling a legal pad with notes and diagrams largely unreadable by anyone other than the scribe. They spoke infrequently.

The pair drove southward in the rain, droplets sizzling and steaming off the hot pavement of Highway 17. On either side of the two-lane road the humidity rose from the wetlands of the ACE Basin, vaporizing on the car's windscreen. Formed and framed by the Ashepoo, Combahee and Edisto Rivers, the preserve was crisscrossed by countless tidal creeks and streams in addition to the main freshwater rivers that gave the basin its name. From the road, the marshlands could be seen disappearing far into the distance.

The great spartina grass wetlands sped past as Quinton asked, "What's our next step, Lake?"

"I am uncertain if we will have any success assisting Thomas," Schmidt said, squinting, his neck craned forward as he peered through the foggy window. "I am a great admirer of his, his academic work, his history with Lumumba . . ." Schmidt's voice trailed off.

"Do you think he has ties with Mobutu?" Quinton asked, keeping his eyes on the slick highway and a firm grip on the steering wheel. "Or has he been out of the trenches too long?"

"Those would be obstacles we might overcome, Daniel, but the truth of the matter is . . ." Schmidt paused. "Mobutu is too strong.

"He may appear to be pressured to hold elections, but he will resist with all the strength and resources at his command." Schmidt continued, "You may recall he renamed himself Mobutu Sese Seko Kuku Ngbendu Wa Za Banga, which roughly translates as 'The All-Powerful Warrior Who goes from Conquest to Conquest, Leaving Fire in His Wake'."

Quinton dared a quick glance over at his partner.

"No, I'm not making that up. I may have missed an adjective or two, but this title is widely known in Zaire," Schmidt said. "And his style of governance has generally been accepted as the genesis of the term *kleptocracy*, which might suggest he has ample reserves in his war chest."

"Let me take a wild stab here and suggest that Fareid is aware of this as well," Quinton surmised.

"He hasn't said as much, but yes, I believe so," Schmidt said. "And, yes, I think Fareid maneuvered Thomas for an introduction to President Bissoula," Schmidt finished, anticipating Quinton's follow-on comment.

"At this point, let me guess: we will be waiting to hear from Fareid in London," Quinton said. "And for the foreseeable future, a campaign strategy for Mr. Kanza will remain a mote in the professor's eye."

"Would like to think otherwise, Daniel, but hopping over to the north side of the Congo River from Kinshasa to Brazzaville appears our absolute best chance to work in Africa.

"And Thomas will help us with building trust between Bissoula and our group." Schmidt concluded.

The car thrummed over the Combahee River Bridge, and Schmidt turned his head west toward the flats where oysters were beginning to appear in clusters along the creek banks as the tide receded. The rain was dissipating, but the mist clung to the far reaches of the marsh. Schmidt could smell the warm and invigorating earthiness of the pluff mud. He looked for stirrings of life in the tall grass, saw none, and returned to staring straight ahead.

CHAPTER FIVE

THE GROUP OF friends that had collected at Emily's Restaurant was too large for the front corner venue, so tables had been joined at the rear of the room and the men sat patiently waiting for Lake Schmidt to arrive.

Schmidt entered through the front door, saw the group at the rear of the restaurant, and raised a finger in recognition. He worked his way between the long bar and the dining tables, nodding at the bartender as he passed. Quinton hooked his foot in a chair rung, pushing out a seat for his friend.

"Good evening, gentlemen. Thank you for coming." Schmidt said, surveying the men seated around the table.

On his left sat Steve Farber, a Beaufort lawyer, successful litigator and part-time novelist. "At the heart of every lawyer lies the wreck of a poet," Farber was fond of quoting. His interest in Africa was long-held, and along with recognition of his literary efforts, Farber aspired to being known one day as "an old Africa hand." He had been awaiting Schmidt's arrival anxiously.

To Farber's left was Mark Adrian, a high-end real estate executive, formerly with Prudential properties. Adrian had been 'right-sized' (he hated the business-correct term) out of an almost-corner office in Atlanta. "Of course," he explained, "the 'right-sizing' started with the more experienced employees and their highly-compensated positions." He was less traveled than the others in the group, but he was hungry, and his large house on Peachtree Battle Road needed maintaining. Being "between opportunities," Adrian was ready to be a wanderer, but not an aimless one. Africa was a stretch for him, but with no alternate prizes looming on the horizon, Adrian was in. "At least, as they say in Texas, I'm leaning forward in the saddle," he concluded.

Completing the circle on Quinton's right, Carey Price inched his glass of bourbon around the table in front of him in small squares, smiling at the assemblage. Carey found most human behavior amusing, including his own, and though he was, or perhaps because he was, "of the Manor born," Price was kind and generous to a fault. He was fiercely religious, but complementing his fervor was a refined appreciation of the great American amber pulled lovingly from Tennessee charcoal vats. "For an Episcopalian, you'd make a good Irish Catholic," Quinton would say to his friend. The hard-drinking Christian felt an ineluctable draw to joining a group headed for the Congo. "Congo, for the love of heaven! If I might travel lightly, I'm already packed. I have a spare toothbrush in my car outside for just such a possibility. We are leaving when?"

Schmidt smiled and rested his hands on the table, as if this were the first day of class, and addressed the group. "For those of you who have an interest in going to Africa, specifically the Congo, there may be an opportunity for us to join together as a group and meet with the President of that new republic, Pascal Bissoula."

Schmidt looked at Quinton, then continued, "We have been granted an interview with him in Brazzaville through the good graces of our friends Fareid Chamoun and Thomas Kanza. As Daniel and I may have mentioned to you when we returned from London, Thomas Kanza's hopes for seeking high office in Zaire have been postponed, but he has made good on his promise to introduce our team to President Bissoula," Schmidt proffered.

"Fareid chooses to refer to our group as a 'delegation'," Quinton joined in. "Of course we represent only ourselves, so the term is applied loosely. It has a nice ring to it though, and sounds like we carry significant tonnage, don't you agree? 'The American Delegation'."

The men around the table looked at Quinton, then back to Dr. Schmidt. Price's grin broadened and he moved his chair closer to the table.

"What are we really going to do over there?" Adrian asked.

"I would suggest we be excursionists, for a start," Farber said, lightly adjusting his wire-rim glasses. "Then learn if there are commercial openings once we have feet on the ground. For me, I would very much like to journal the trip, and perhaps send dispatches back for publication in the *New York Times*. Or failing that, the *Beaufort Gazette*." Farber took a short pull on his scotch.

"Failing that, I know your wife would be glad to get a letter," Quinton added.

Farber grinned into his drink and nodded. Pulling a fountain pen from his jacket pocket, he waved it at Quinton, drawing an exclamation point in the air. "*Tu sais, on ne sais jamais!* You know, you never know!"

"So, Steve, it would be safe to say you're not planning to feed the little Farbers or feather the out-years with what might happen as a result of the 'openings'?" Adrian asked. "To me, that this kind of pay day is even a possibility counts for something." *And now, this possibility is all I've got*, he thought.

"There are no guarantees," Schmidt answered for him, "just as in any enterprise. The risk/reward ratio is not a promising one, and certainly not one to count on if you plan to subsidize a meandering journey through undergraduate school for the young'n. But, that said, what a journey it will be."

Quinton reached into his pocket, pulled out maps and background papers on West Africa that he handed to the other men, and said, "Not exactly a journey to a theme park either, although it may turn out to be an E-ticket ride.

"The trick," he said, clearing his throat "is not to wander too far from the herd, stay with our government minders (they'll be Bissoula's men), and keep a wad of Congolese Francs—CFAs (or Ceefas as they call them)—in your pocket." Quinton paused. "State Department makes it sound worse than it is," he added, and looked at the Delegation for reaction. There wasn't much of one from any of the soon-to-be excursionists.

"Keep your passport with you at all times and in your front pocket. You will be separated from it for a brief period while checking into the hotel, but otherwise stay attached to it," Quinton continued.

"The Embassy will be notified we are in Brazzaville, and what we're up to," Schmidt said. "The Ambassador and CIA Chief of Station, who is often the 'Political Officer,' or occasionally the 'Economic Officer,' will be particularly interested in our meeting with the President."

"As will the French, and particularly our new friends-to-be, the field men at ELF Aquitaine," Quinton said. "They will be the lying, shoulder-shrugging, surly, hotel-watching gentlemen with silk shirts on their backs and larceny in their hearts. Did I overstate that, Lake?"

"Not by a lot, Daniel."

Quinton pushed back in his chair, looked at the group, then saw a swirl of color brush through the front door and head for the hallway that led to the changing room behind the bar. The figure vanished momentarily, but petite fingers latched onto the doorframe, and a tussle of honey-colored hair and a pair of green eyes reappeared sideways from the door. Molly allowed just her face to protrude from the opening, gave Quinton her signature double eyebrow raise, then melted through the doorway like a lemon drop.

Quinton closed his eyes and exhaled slowly, unable to shake the image of the woman who had become a solar flare in his otherwise bleak atmosphere. He dropped some bills on the table, headed for the back room, but then changed direction and followed the other men out of the restaurant. He reached his truck across the street and climbed in.

CHAPTER SIX

THE NEWLY APPOINTED Minister of Agriculture brushed the dust from the lapels and trouser fronts of his blue serge suit, and settled in behind his expansive mahogany desk. The office was modest, he thought, but the freshly painted lettering on the door announced to those entering that this was the office of Pascal Bissoula, *Ministre d'Agriculture*, and the gold-framed colorized lithograph of President Alphonse Massamba-Debat looked down approvingly upon his appointee. A modest office was quite secondary, Bissoula reasoned, when these more significant omens were considered and appreciated.

From a botanist to Minister, Bissoula mused. He straightened his small calendar on the bronze stand and marked today, his first in office. February 25, 1963. He looked out of one of two jalousied windows on the far side of the room and sighed; a row of eucalyptus trees swayed in unison in the breeze on the far side of the courtyard, and they annoyed His Excellency. "They drink too much water," he said to the empty chairs opposite him.

The clacking of the secretary's heels resonated on the linoleum and down the plain gray walls of the hallway leading to the Minister's office. The door to the room was slightly ajar, so Minister Bissoula was aware of the approaching messenger before her light knock landed on the doorframe. *This does not bode well for the Minister of less than a year,* he thought. Usually Mlle. Moulon would telephone from the outer office with news of visitors, or troubling accounts of adverse weather, or crop production reports. In recent months, however, her visits seemed to occur more often, and the messages were increasingly tinged more with political intrigue and less with crop yield data. When no one else was present, she began addressing His Excellency as Pascal, a breech Bissoula corrected twice, but Mlle. Moulon had persisted and emerged victorious.

"The President's driver is outside, Pascal," Mlle. Moulon said quietly. "I was advised to inform you that when you visit with Mr. President, a briefcase would not be required."

Minister Bissoula came around the desk, which during his tenure received ever-more-energetically-applied layers of polish, enabling the Minister to slide assignments across the gleaming surface with a mere finger flick. As he moved closer to Mlle. Moulon he could smell her scent, and he lightly brushed her back as he swung on his overcoat. She smoothed the shoulders of the Minister's coat as he stood facing the door, smiling to herself, pleased with the effect she was having on him. *The pathway to fulfillment runs through the halls of power,* she reminded herself. She held the door for him, but not stepping too far back, arranging another opportunity for him to be near her.

"I will drive my own car, Mlle. Moulon," Bissoula announced loudly enough for anyone within eavesdropping distance to hear. "Inform the driver." He had no intention of taking his own car. *This may buy some time if I'm followed*, he thought.

When Bissoula arrived at the front of the Ministers' office building, the driver had opened the back door and waited for his passenger at the side of the black Gaz-13 Chaika limousine. The Russian-made car was a gift to the Congolese government from the Soviets, and was a favorite of KGB operatives. The large rear seat made it easy for them to simply drive by "suspicious" comrades and pull them inside.

Bissoula motioned the driver to stop. "It is a privilege to be driven by the President's driver, and I gratefully accept the kind offer," he said. "But if I may be permitted, I would prefer to ride in the front seat." The driver nodded knowingly; this was a practice he had seen before. An assassin would normally target his first round at the rear seat position, and although just a fraction of a second would pass before the next round was squeezed off, it might be just enough time for the alerted passenger in front to find the floor.

The driver closed the back door then opened the passenger side front door for the Minister. Now, reluctantly more alert, he swept the area for anything remotely resembling a gun barrel. He adjusted his Ray Ban aviators and stepped smartly to the driver's side, annoyed a chance for a quick cigarette had been lost. "Always better when they sit in back," he mumbled to himself. "Always."

The office of the President stood in the interior of the Palais de la Nation, previously the vault in the center of the national bank. Its double doors were moderately ornate and made to appear impenetrable by the Presidential Guards who flanked either side. Their weapons were held at ease, but the AK-47s' banana clip magazines were attached, and the uniformed pair was decidedly non-ceremonial.

President Massamba-Dabat's personal secretary, Monsieur Cristophe Masena, walked with Minister Bissoula toward the entrance of the presidential office. He nodded to the camouflaged duo and then knocked lightly on the door, turning the handle at the same time.

"*Monsieur le Presidente, Ministre Bissoula,*" Masena announced.

"Pascal! Please, please come in," the President said. "And *merci,* Christophe," he said, nodding and dismissing his aide.

The door closed behind Masena, and the President motioned for Bissoula to join him on the sofa beneath the heavily curtained window. Bissoula glanced quickly out, and adjusted his position on the couch to minimize the firing angle from the garden outside.

"No, no. Sit closer, Pascal," the President said. Bissoula moved toward the President slightly. "As you may have imagined, I must make changes, dramatic changes in my cabinet, if I am to stay in power." Bissoula nodded, and looked again into the garden.

The two men sat locked in conversation for over an hour; a light breeze, carrying the slightest fragrance of the Jacaranda blooming in the courtyard, wafted through the minutely open window. Bissoula decided that today was not the day a bullet would come through the glass. It would come instead from Alphonse Massamba-Debat.

Mlle. Moulon came running toward the front chamber of the Minister's Building, looking frantically for her boss. The driver of the limousine had just arrived at the curb near the front door, and Moulon could see there was no passenger in the rear of the black sedan.

"Where is *Ministre* Bissoula, where is he?"

"He is no longer," the driver said. "But *Prime Minister* Bissoula is here in the front of my limousine, *c'est ca.*

Mlle. Moulon scurried toward the car, and the front door opened. Prime Minister Bissoula raised a finger in caution, and Mlle. Moulon slowed to a walk, and said, "Prime Minister? Oh, Monsieur Bissoula, how wonderful! Your family will be so proud! It was destined."

Bissoula closed the sedan door and buttoned his coat against the evening wind. He addressed Mlle. Moulon quietly. "My meeting with the President was entirely different from the one I expected. Instead of a termination with a bullet, or a dismissal with the wave of a hand, here I am." Opening his arms wide, he presented the new Prime Minister.

Mlle. Moulon thought for a moment the gesture was intended for her embrace, but realized quickly, as Bissoula gazed far off into the gathering dusk, it was not for her but the political universe his arms were spread.

"We must get to work, Mlle. Moulon," the Prime Minister said, and began striding purposefully toward the white stone building.

CHAPTER SEVEN

T HE FIVE MEN with various backgrounds, but singleness of purpose and destination, stood in line at the ticket counter for Air Afrique in the terminal at JFK International Airport. The American Delegation stood patiently and watched with interest the proceedings that played out in a great hubbub before them: the carry-on luggage and baggage to be checked by their fellow passengers were astonishing in their variety, weight and girth.

A passenger agent on the far left of the counter was arguing with an African man dressed in a bold yellow-and-green-patterned garb of many folds, containing at least ten yards of material. It was imaginatively tucked and swirled, and stayed in place through no small feat of personal engineering. He was exasperated in the extreme that the agent wouldn't allow him to check his "baggage," an entire automobile muffler system. The exhaust assembly, when stood on end, towered over the traveler and the bewildered, but persevering, ticketer.

In the check-in line ahead of the Delegation, waiting for their opportunity to check baggage, returning visitors stood with their acquisitions from the vast markets and warehouses of America. Their suitcases had castored wheels and were the size of refrigerators. When pushed forward, the behemoths strayed quickly from the intended path while their owners struggled mightily to keep them on course. The colorful wear; the perspiring efforts of the freight bearers; the hullabaloo raised by debates ongoing in second and sometimes third languages created a chaotic, but for the most part agreeable scene. For the travelers coursing through the veins and arteries of the departure terminal, the exhilaration of soon heading off into the night skies over the North Atlantic was contagious.

Quinton and Schmidt shared a brief look after they took in the reaction of their associates to the unfolding theatre: Farber smiling and scribbling furiously in a steno pad, Adrian blinking behind his tortoise shell glasses, and Price fascinated and entertained by the human comedy. *The journey is well and truly underway, and 'the game is afoot,'* Schmidt reflected. Completing the thought to himself, he muttered: "Let's hope the arrival home is equally energizing."

As the Air Afrique Airbus 310 climbed into the dark sky over Long Island and was vectored to join its assigned track over the Atlantic, the man seated across the aisle from Mark Adrian tapped a cigarette out of his pack and lit up. Adrian stared at him with surprise. Smoke curled from the passenger's lips, and then was exhaled in a stream toward the overhead. The chagrined American looked forward then aft for the flight attendant. She saw his raised hand and grudgingly walked toward him from the aft-section galley, where she had planned on staying unnoticed, unhailed, and therefore unrequired to be responsive.

"*Oui, Monsieur?*" she asked, making an indifferent effort to hide her annoyance.

"I was supposed to be in a non-smoking seat," Adrian said, pointing out the smoker with a stare.

"You are, Monsieur," she smiled.

"What about him?" again turning his gaze toward the offending puffer.

"He, of course, is in a smoking seat," she shrugged. "May I bring you some water?"

"Suffering Moses," Adrian said to himself, shaking his head. "No, not right now," he answered the flight attendant.

Lake Schmidt, mindful of the economics of self-funded travel, had purchased special rate tickets for his colleagues aboard Air Afrique. A bonus feature of the exclusive arrangement was not only a refueling stop in Abidjan, Ivory Coast, but also a 24 hour spend-the-night at the travel agency's staff-recommended, two-and-half star, all-inclusive resort. "Getting the dust of Africa on your boots gradually," Schmidt described it. Quinton had suggested other travel options, but was unsuccessful in convincing the budget-minded Schmidt.

"Abidjan should be interesting," Schmidt had responded to Quinton's objections.

"Hope so, Lake."

The airliner slowed, nosed over slightly, and began its descent into Felix Houphouet-Boigny International Airport in Abidjan. The change in pitch of the Airbus awakened Quinton. The sun was up and bright and streamed through the windows of those who chose to slide the sunscreens up, much to the annoyance of passengers still napping. Quinton looked to see if his friends were awake and alert. They were.

As the big jet banked left, the airfield came into view, filling the windows on the down wing side of the aircraft.

The tarmac was empty save two other Air Afrique jetliners; there were no small private aircraft. Two fire and rescue trucks sat parked at mid-field, and the terminal roof gleamed white, the airport buildings squared to the ramp. Quinton wondered if the crash trucks were actually manned.

As the aircraft came to a stop, passengers rustled and stretched and began collecting their belongings. Over the cabin speakers the lead flight attendant droned on in French about matters of vital importance, none of which held any interest to the travelers. Schmidt caught the eye of each of the team members over the heads of deplaning passengers, and motioned with his hands for all to meet at the base of the air stairs. The doors opened, and the first breath of Africa, hot, humid and vibrant, filled the cabin.

Steve Farber was the last to join the group on the steamy asphalt; he was absorbing every sensory sliver of the moment for later transcription to his steno pad. Armed men, he noticed, were stationed along the ramp to ensure disembarking visitors would proceed toward no destination other than the terminal. The assault rifles hanging by their sides instead of reassuring the tourists, as perhaps was the intent of the Minister of Tourism, simply made the soldiers look menacing and sinister. Carey Price smiled and waved at one, whose only reaction was to turn slightly to inspect the next weary-but-alert voyager in line.

Inside the terminal, Lake Schmidt had surged ahead of the group and plunged into the jostling crowd of Ivoirians to select and retain a 'fixer.'

"My fren'!" "My fren', over here!" "Engleese? American? Canadienne? I speak all!" "Very cheap, very clean!" "America number one country!"

Schmidt looked high over the heads of the reaching and grabbing supplicants, knowing that once eye contact was made it was as good as over; the sighted one would never let go. Lacking any meaningful referrals, and so relying on his statistical acumen (his doctoral dissertation was a data-driven explanation of voting trends in urban elections, a weighty manuscript Quinton promised to read first chance he got), Schmidt pointed and looked at the young man with the brightest face and cleanest tee shirt, the one that said, "NIKE Just Do It."

"You," Schmidt said, pointing again.

The young man stepped forward, elbowing and fending off the other suitors who hadn't given up entirely, but who saw chance of success rapidly declining. In moments, most of the unchosen were off in pursuit of fresh quarry.

"Of course! I can see in your face you gentleman, one who choose wisely!" the young man said. "I am Eddie. How many in your party? Do you have the womens?"

Schmidt looked back over the heads of the heaving crowd of employment seekers, airport officials and baggage searchers, and saw no familiar faces, no trace of the American Delegation. "We will need two taxis," he said not looking at Eddie, but continuing his sweep of the terminal in search of the now missing excursionists. "Please help me with the luggage," and Schmidt moved toward the baggage carrousels, still searching to pick out anything familiar—a coat, a ball cap, a pair of glasses, a gesture. He saw none.

Back on the other side of the "Customs/Douane" placard, the remainder of the team had gathered around Carey Price, Daniel Quinton, and a camouflaged official who held Price tightly by the arm. "No photographs! No photographs!" he was saying forcefully to the now bewildered American.

"Daniel, I was just taking a picture of the beach sign that said 'Playa Loco'...." I thought it would make a good shot!" Price pleaded, holding tightly to his 35mm Nikon.

"At an African airport there are no fun shots," Quinton explained, trying to insert himself between the two. The official was having none of it.

"To them, and to the President, this is like a military base. Remember," Quinton said, continuing to dance his way between the antagonists, "there are a lot of sendoffs and departures here. This is where the overthrown government, what's left of it anyway, makes a dash to a country that won't extradite. Cash helps, of course." Quinton shuffled left then right. "For that reason, air terminals are tightly controlled."

At this point the guard had had enough, reached around Quinton, and pulled Price by the arm, pointing to a side door. "Communist! You are Communist! Come with me!"

"Hold on, sir! We are an American Delegation travelling at the invitation of the President of Congo-Brazzaville. Where one member goes, we all go!" Quinton announced, rounding up Farber and Adrian and herding them toward the door through which the guard and the now unamused Carey Price had just disappeared.

"We can't lose him; let's go! Stay together," Quinton enjoined, picking up the pace and trying to keep the two in sight.

The long, concrete hallway was unlit, moldy, and stank of the apprehension and anxiety of the intimidated. As Quinton expected, it led to an interrogation room into which his friend and the enforcer were entering.

"Mr. Price is a member of our delegation, and we can clear this up very quickly, with our sincere apologies," Quinton said, ushering the remaining delegates into the room. He addressed a large perspiring man with an open collar and more brass devices on his epaulets than the other uniformed men in the room. Price was instructed to take a seat opposite the senior officer at the metal table. He still held firmly to his camera, his leather satchel, and his belief in the goodness of mankind.

"You are forbidden to photograph any area of this airport." The Commandante spoke slowly and directly to Price.

"I am so sorry, sir, I was entirely unaware of the restriction, and I can assure you . . . ." Price began.

"Take the camera," the Commandante motioned to one of his subordinates.

Quinton stepped forward and grabbed the Nikon from Price, saying to the large man, "This was a breach, Excellency, and will not happen again." He popped the back of the camera open, pulled out the roll of 35 mm film, and placed the curling remains on the desk.

"But those were photos of this beautiful country taken during our approach, and . . ." Price protested. Quinton placed his hand on Price's shoulder, adding quietly, "Lose the film or lose the film *and* the camera, Carey. Easy choice."

"With your kind permission, Excellency," Quinton said, now motioning the group to start moving toward the door. Metal chairs scraped on the linoleum floor. "We would like to rejoin Professor Schmidt, who awaits outside. We are scheduled to check in with the American Embassy and begin our tour of Abidjan and the Cote d'Ivoire."

Quinton continued, "Most of us have never left the borders of our own country and are unfamiliar with important regulations, regulations you, of course, must enforce. Your understanding of our indiscretion is a clear signal your government encourages foreign investment. Your kind treatment will not be forgotten, and your cordiality communicated to the Ambassador, here and in Brazzaville."

The Commandante raised his eyelids almost imperceptibly, but remained seated. As he had throughout the interview, he continued to drum his gold-ringed right forefinger on the desk. A flash of recognition had breezed across Quinton's face, but disappeared. When he spoke to the Commandante, he focused on the man's forehead, straining to avoid any hint that he recognized the soldier from the roadblock of almost a decade ago.

The Commandante was unimpressed with the group, and even less impressed with his chances of parlaying the detention of travelers headed to the U.S. Embassy into something worthwhile. *Had Sergeant Nguoba cut one out of the herd, it might have been amusing for a while, maybe even profitable,* he thought. *Now, however, it is time for lunch.*

"Obey our laws, and enjoy our country." He pointed at the now deflated Sergeant who had initially detained Price, and waved at him to escort the stumbling gaggle of unimportance from his interrogation room.

When the door to the interrogation room closed, the Commandante picked up the receiver and placed a call to Brazzaville. "Danou. Georges Danou, please.

"'Allo, Danou. I will be brief. There is an American group here in Abidjan, but travelling your way. They will be very troublesome. Your friends will not appreciate their intentions. Any help I can offer, I am willing."

The voice at the other end was barely audible. "I see. If that changes, please recall my business remains a cash operation." He hung up.

Dragging behind the group with Sgt. Nguoba, Quinton stopped in front of the Men's Room. "Will you stay with my friends, please? I must use the restroom. I have not been well at all," Quinton said, wincing and massaging his abdomen. The soldier dismissed him with a wave toward the restroom door, shook his head, and then turned to follow the others.

Quinton waited for the soldier to turn the corner, then ducked across the hall into the Ladies' Room. Once inside the tiled space, Quinton quickly entered the stall, slammed the slide closed, and surveyed the enclosure. From his wallet, he pulled six crisp $100 bills. He folded them in half, then again, creasing them with his thumbnail to make them as tight as a calling card.

The trim piece that joined the two sheets of linoleum on the wall came loose when Quinton plied it with his small penknife. He carefully placed each folded bill about four inches apart, then hammered the trim board back into the wall with his fist.

Running his hand along the trim, Quinton felt it was smooth and looked undisturbed. He opened the stall door and left the restroom to rejoin the group.

Schmidt spotted Quinton ahead of the group and waved, shooting a quizzical sideways look at his partner. Quinton gave a quick shrug and shook his head, then proceeded to help the others gather up their luggage. They joined Schmidt, who stood by two unmistakably related Ivoirian men. The pair wore tee shirts and faded yellow linen pants, badly misshapen at the knees. Brown woven toeless sandals finished off their outfits. The taller of the two stepped forward quickly to welcome the Americans. "You are gentlemen of distinction. And luck," he added. "You have contracted with Eddie and his cousin to take care of all your needs while you are here."

The two drivers loaded baggage and Americans into battered Peugeots, strapping the larger cases to the roof with a creative array of bungee cords, twine, and hemp rope. Thus bound, the taxis took on the look of dung beetles, lacking only a starter animal dropping with which they could begin to tumble. The cars pulled away from the curb and lurched forward into the dusty afternoon, Eddie in the vanguard beetle.

The two-car convoy had gone no farther than Boulevard Valery Giscard d'Estaing when the lead taxi pulled over to the shoulder, sending rocks and dust wheeling into the air.

"Eddie's renegotiating the fare, I'm guessing" Quinton said, seated in the front seat of the second taxi.

In and around the forward taxi, a debate had begun, and the participants were becoming more agitated with each passing minute and each passing car. Quinton climbed from his taxi, as Farber and Schmidt exited theirs.

"Eddie, you are a good man," Farber began, inserting himself into the contentious stew. "You told us so yourself. You also told us we were fortunate to have retained the services of you and your excellent cousin."

Eddie leaned against the door of the taxi, his palms pressed into his eye sockets. Farber continued, "At the airport, Dr. Schmidt made you an offer, Eddie, and you accepted. To change that contract all parties must agree, and we do NOT agree, so changing the terms would make that contract null and void, and our set price goes out the window."

Quinton added quietly, "And Eddie, we are prepared to unload the bags right here."

Eddie stared back in amazement "What you talking!? What it mean!? Nollenvoid?"

Farber said, "Eddie, my friend, we will pay you what we promised and no more."

"But your baggage . . ." Eddie's voice trailed off. He had lost the skirmish and with a show of much-practiced sadness, mounted the lead taxi and pouted his way back onto the Boulevard. Eddie's cousin sat quietly during the exchange, gripping the fat rubber-knurled steering wheel ever tighter, frequently shifting his bony frame on the wooden prayer-bead looking seat cover. The procession was rejoined and the dung beetles were once again moving forward.

The sign for the resort swung lazily behind a huge African oil palm. *En Dernier Ressort* the lettering had boldly pronounced some years ago when it was freshly painted. Locally crafted and artfully done, both had suffered the inevitable beating from the relentless central African sun.

The group gathered their belongings from the ground next to the taxis where they had been unceremoniously deposited. Schmidt paid Eddie, counting each banknote with care and precision as his cousin watched anxiously from the safe haven of his driver's seat.

While Eddie held his hand out for the cash, he kept his eye on Quinton. "*J'aime pas ta bouille,*" he said to himself, "*Va niquier toi-meme!*" jutting his jaw toward Quinton.

"What'd he say?" Quinton asked when Schmidt joined him in dragging their bags into the lobby.

"First, he didn't like your face, and second," Schmidt thought for a moment, "and second, he suggested something not physiologically possible."

"Very nice. Suggest we all count our bags . . ."

After a quick tally of the luggage, the pair lifted their belongings and struggled through the heavy carved lobby doors, held open by an elderly Ivoirian, crisply turned out in his heavily starched doorman's ensemble. The lobby was open on all sides. Plants of every description adorned the rafters, hung from the walls; were placed about the floors and gardens in the interior courtyard garden. Heavy wooden pillars, full trunks of exotic trees extracted from the rain forest when that seemed a good idea, buttressed the lobby ceiling. The hallway that led to the dining area at the back of the hotel was similarly constructed.

A humid breath of air swirled lightly through the open area. The scents were fragrant and unfamiliar—exotic aromas wafted unmistakably from the resort kitchen's wood fire: curry, cumin, paprika, and what guests would learn later were hot harissa, isinongo sama zula, and berbere.

"Not entirely unpleasant," Schmidt said, surveying the verdant lobby and surrounds, his nose raised to inhale and appreciate the moment. He turned to address the group. "Gentlemen, dinner has been arranged in the back garden." He raised his right arm and pointed with all four fingers in the direction of the long hallway. "Seating at eight o'clock. Dress: tropical evening casual. Denim, regardless of cost or label, strongly discouraged. See you there."

A light rain had begun to titillate the palm fronds overhanging the dinner table set for the Americans. *Pit . . . pit, pit . . .* the drops started slowly, then *pit pit pit.* The raindrops beat intermittently on the overhead palms and the elephant ear leaves and hibiscus plants that embraced the courtyard dining area. A long wooden table cut from an enormous tropical tree was centered in the space. The concrete floor under it ran out to the adjoining gardens. Windowless, doorless, and framed only by other single tree columns, the dining area was entirely open, designed for weather that was largely unchanging throughout the year.

Around the long table, chairs and place settings for twelve were arranged. Four wine glasses fanned out from the right of each diner toward the massive centerpiece of ferns, hibiscus blossoms, and Birds of Paradise. The manager and host, Robert K. Ndoullah, stood at the head of the table awaiting the guests. With a critical eye and a finely tuned sense of propriety, he surveyed the perfection of the dinner setting stretched out before him. To his satisfaction, he found nothing amiss.

"Please, please, my friends," Mr. Ndoullah said to the arriving guests, waving them toward the table. With his right hand, he indicated the diner, and with his left, the diner's assigned seat. "Professor Schmidt," he motioned to Lake, "please accept the seat of the grandfather, the patriarch, at the end of the table."

Schmidt demurred unconvincingly and took his seat, noting that each member of the delegation sat next to an empty chair. Then, on a scarcely detectable signal from Mr. Ndoullah, five attractive and colorfully attired young ladies glided in from what seemed like all quarters of the garden to take up residence at the table. Smiling, and occasionally giggling behind manicured little hands, they appeared genuinely pleased to be invited to the festivities, the open-ended nature of their duties notwithstanding.

Light conversation began as the first course was served, but before the trenching began in earnest, Carey Price asked for everyone's attention. Quinton and Schmidt exchanged a glance.

"Would y'all be so kind and join hands to pray with me before this bountiful meal we are about to receive?" Price reached out to take the hand of his somewhat-taken-aback dinner partners, who took their cue from the direct gaze of Mr. Ndoullah and closed their eyes. The circle was soon unbroken, heads were bowed, and Price began:

"Heavenly Father, we thank you for this evening in Abidjan and the gifts you are about to set before us," he began. The girls sneaked a peak at each other.

"And for your tender mercies throughout our lives, we give you thanks," Price prayed. From the youngest, at the other end of the table, a soft "Amen." From the other girls, muffled tittering.

Price carried on undaunted, "Where we travel throughout this beautiful continent, and with these beautiful people," more giggles, "keep us in your protective care."

Another hopeful "Amen," then more tittering. But now a severe and penetrating glare from Mr. Ndoullah subdued the mirth and young heads returned to where they were directed, in a posture of respect.

"In Your name we pray," Price raised his head, looked at the young girls around the table, grinned and said, "Now!"

"Amen!" They shouted in unison, and with unrestrained glee.

Mr. Ndoullah took in a deep breath, exhaled, and then, smiling, stood to tend to the needs of his guests.

"Runs a tight ship, our host," Quinton said.

"He does indeed," Schmidt responded.

After dinner and rounds of well-meaning toasts and salutes to the nobility of all humankind, the two men had moved to the wickered chairs on the veranda.

Schmidt added, "And his brother Youssef, I'm told, runs a very tight ship at the Ministry of Justice."

"So I've heard, Lake. A severe beating awaits those who don't forward the full percentage of bribes and shakedowns to His Excellency." Quinton looked off into the night. "So, I'm told anyway."

Schmidt turned in his chair to get a better read on his partner in the evening light. Quinton continued staring into the darkening tree line. "What happened back there? At the airport?" Schmidt asked.

Quinton's gaze didn't change. He took a breath, then said, "Lake, sometimes Fate, or God, or Allah, or the Universe or whatever you want to call Why Things Turn Out the Way They Do, lines up on one's side to even a score. And it will surprise you because the score seems so goddamned lopsided you think it can never be squared.

"Today is not the first time I've come across the Commandante, the goon who detained Carey and interrogated us at the airport. You didn't get a chance to see him, but he's a nasty piece of work." Quinton flexed his right hand and lightly rubbed his forearm while he spoke. "Had we not stuck together in the sweat box, I am absolutely certain he would have shaken us down for everything we had that wasn't hidden in a personal cavity."

"Let me venture a guess here, my friend," Schmidt said quietly. "Commandante was involved in the 'runaway hedge trimmer' incident when you were injured years ago," Schmidt looked at Quinton, who quickly stopped massaging his hand. "And I suspect there was a lot more damage inflicted during the episode than just that," Schmidt said nodding toward Quinton's right arm.

Quinton continued to look into the darkening sky and didn't respond. Across the veranda, Robert Ndoullah guided the clean up staff, and Quinton turned to watch him tend the herd. "Curious how both brothers ended up in the hospitality business," Quinton said. "Trust they've stayed close over the years, and that they happily share information. Information that helps them 'be the best they can be' in their positions of responsibility.

"Lake, will you please excuse me for just a minute? I'd like to thank Mr. Ndoullah for his efforts tonight."

Schmidt watched as Quinton weaved his way through the dining tables and chairs that had been moved randomly to make way for the cleaners. Ndoullah looked up as Quinton approached. He smiled broadly and extended both hands in greeting. Quinton did the same, and they shook hands as if they were Heads of State appearing before the press corps.

"Mr. Ndoullah, this has been the most memorable of evenings, and you have been the host beyond compare."

Ndoullah bowed in acknowledgment and said, "I am so delighted you and your friends have enjoyed your introduction to my country. And my offer to enhance your stay in any way imaginable stands. In any way . . ."

"Thank you. I know you would." Quinton paused, then said, "I must tell you this evening has been in stark contrast to our reception at the airport. It became very expensive for our group today. In order to spare my colleagues, I paid the "entry fee" of $600 per person demanded by the Commandante. But that is not your problem, and I regret bringing it up." Quinton began rubbing his forehead in apology. "Mr. Ndoullah, please forgive me, this evening will be the memory we will take away from today."

"What time did your group clear through the airport?" Ndoullah asked, his face grim.

"Around midday, but please, this matter should never have been mentioned. Tonight was perfect. All your touches were thoughtful and much appreciated by our delegation."

"For that, I am pleased," Ndoullah replied. "But do you remember the Commandante's name, or anything else that might identify him?"

Quinton paused, then said, "No I'm sorry, not really. He was very intimidating. Guess that's why I thought it strange he would use the Ladies' Room." Quinton again rubbed his forehead apologetically. "That, of course, has nothing to do with anything. I so regret mentioning this. It was an inconvenience, no more. Tonight will be the centerpiece of our visit to Abidjan."

"You are so kind to say so. But, if you will please excuse me, I must make a telephone call." Ndoullah grasped Quinton's arm in a departing gesture, then headed for his office.

Quinton watched him enter, then close the door as he switched on his desk lamp. He picked up the receiver and impatiently hammered the telephone cradle, waiting for the operator to respond. Quinton could see his initial exchange was brief, and that the conversation that followed was animated and angry.

Schmidt had settled contentedly on the veranda, but turned in his chair to watch the interaction between his friend and Ndoullah. He saw Quinton standing perfectly still, hands clasped behind him, watching the man on the phone as if he were watching surgery from an observation deck. Quinton returned to the terrace and the calm and comfort of the large fanback chair he had just left.

"Delightful evening, Professor," Quinton said quietly. He looked at Schmidt then turned to look up at the blue-black of the night sky. For long minutes he said nothing, then added, "Just delightful."

CHAPTER EIGHT

M INISTER BISSOULA RESTED the newspaper he was reading on the breakfast table next to his coffee cup and empty plate. He wiped his mouth with the white cloth napkin that had been set to his left, and looked at the front-page article, this time from over the top of his glasses:

August 5, 1968

Brazzaville—Today, in the capital of Congo-Brazzaville, Marien Ngouabi announced the formation of the National Revolutionary Council (CNR), which he will head. Many observers see this as a direct challenge to the Massamba-Debat government.

Lieutenant Ngouabi, along with Second Lieutenant Eyabo, was arrested on orders of the President on July 29th of this year for insubordination. His arrest provoked discontent among the military, and on July 31st, two days later, Ngouabi was freed by soldiers of the garrison where he was jailed.

Bissoula looked up from the table and rubbed his temples. This did not bode well for President Massamba-Debat. Worse yet, it did not portend well for the continuing prestige and prosperity of those in his government. Bissoula pushed back from the table and walked across the room to the sideboard where he picked up the telephone.

"Mlle. Moulon," he said, then corrected himself. "My apologies, Mme. . . ."

"My married name is Mme. Badoun, Pascal," the voice on the other end of the line reminded him. "It has been for almost a year."

"Of course. I am sorry," Bissoula said. "Please have the car brought to the back courtyard. Quickly, Marie!"

In the office of the President, Pascal Bissoula sat with Alphonse Massamba-Debat and his two closest allies, Georges Bufasse and Alfred Raoul. When a coalition was cobbled together in the summer of 1966 to keep Massamba-Debat in power, Bissoula was asked to step down as Prime Minister (doing so reluctantly, but loyally), to be replaced by Raoul. Bissoula continued in government as Senior Advisor, but his ambitions were not to go quietly into the dark night, especially with the brigand Ngouabi making noises around the Presidential Palace.

"The CNR has so diluted the authority of this office, I have become nothing more than wallpaper," the President said to those in the room. "The Council has nominal support among the people, but they have the backing of the army, which ultimately decides who has the authority to head the government."

"Alfred, my friend, you will serve as acting head of state when I resign tomorrow."

The three men gathered around the President looked at one another in astonishment, but not in disbelief. They had seen this coming in August when the Council had been formed. With the backing of the military, the CNR had had immediate validity and clout. Bissoula, Raoul and Bufasse stood and waited for Masamba-Dubat to stand. He waved the men out with a tired gesture. He would spend his few remaining hours as President alone.

The following day, September 4, 1968, Alfred Raoul began his short tenure as Head of State, serving until the last day of the year. On December 31ˢᵗ, 1968, the National Revolutionary Council became the country's supreme authority, and Marien Ngouabi, as head of the CNR, assumed the presidency. Pascal Bissoula slipped quietly back into the post of a minor minister in the leftist government, until he was suspended from political activity from 1969 to 1971. In 1973, Bissoula reappeared on the Central Committee of the Congolese Workers Party.

Four years later, in March 1977, Marien Ngouabi was assassinated by what was described as a 'suicidal commando.' Later in that same year, persons accused of taking part in the assassination were tried and some of them executed, including former President Alphonse Massamba-Debat.

Pascal Bissoula was implicated in the assassination, but did not receive the death penalty. Instead he was sentenced to life imprisonment.

In 1979, Bissoula was released from prison, but forced to live in exile in France, where he remained for twelve years. A return to academic life landed Bissoula a teaching position at the University of Paris, where he lectured in botany. By the beginning of 1990 Professor Bissoula had worked for UNESCO in Paris, and later in Nairobi.

Never fully divested of his intense desire to participate in Congolese politics, Bissoula remained connected to political movements in the country. Communism, and for that matter Marxist socialism of all stripes, had run its course in Africa; a groundswell of democratic political ideas was gaining traction across the continent and among the people of the Congo. Pascal Bissoula rose to the forefront of Congolese expatriates who are promoting government of, by, and for the people.

He returned to Brazzaville, Congo in late 1990.

The transitional period of government that began with the February—June, 1991, National Conference was near its end; Denis Sassou-Nguesso had been the provisional President, but fell into disfavor after a controversial attempt at holding a local election. Then, in the first national election, Bissoula's name was placed on the presidential ballot representing the Pan African Union for Social Democracy. His nearest political rival, and bitter enemy, was Bernard Kolelas of the Congolese Movement for Democracy and Integral Development. In Congolese politics 'political rival' and 'bitter enemy' should more appropriately be combined into one word; to use both phrases is quite redundant.

Additionally, in these groundbreaking times, a candidate had much to do with naming his own political party. In addition to the Pan African Union and the Congolese Movement, Rally for Democracy and Social Progress was one; Rally for Democracy and Development, another. Energize the voting public with an inspirational message, the party branding seemed to say.

CHAPTER NINE

THE SUITE AT the M'Bamou Palace in Brazzaville overlooked the Congo River, and from Pascal Bissoula's vantage point in the room, he could see the city of Kinshasa.

"The ballots have been counted . . ." Marie Badoun announced, entering the room. She had almost said 'Pascal' until she noticed Mme. Bissoula and Pierre Dinongo, Bissoula's senior advisor, at the far side of the room. "Monsieur Bissoula, it is now between you and Kolelas!"

Dinongo stepped forward, "Our support was strong in the regions of Niari, Bouenza, and Lekoumou going into the first round, but how did we fare in Brazzaville, Mme. Badoun?"

"Kolelas won a plurality, but only 30%," Badoun said.

Bissoula looked at Dinongo, then turned and looked out over the river. "We need help with the capital, Pierre."

"Sassou-Nguesso finished well in Brazzaville, but the rest of the country? Not so well," Dinongo said. "He has been eliminated from the second round, so he will be willing to support the likely winner." Dinongo motioned toward Bissoula. "As you know Pascal, it will not be without cost."

"I know, my friend, but I also know the truth of 'woe to the man who helps another man to power'!" Bissoula stole a quick glance toward Marie Badoun, then turned to his wife. "Would you care to dine with the next President of the Republic of the Congo, my dear?"

"Only if you will take my arm, Pascal," Mme. Bissoula replied, offering her left arm.

"Keep me apprised of your discussions with Sassou-Nguesso's people. Do not let him think he is the only lever we might pull," Bissoula cautioned.

Dinongo nodded, and Mme. Badoun picked up the bedroom phone to reserve the private dining room as the Bissoula's moved arm-in-arm to the door. Mme. Badoun watched the couple leave and, with Dinongo lost in thought, moved toward the window. She watched them until they disappeared.

The mahogany desk needed a bit of polish to return it to its former luster when Minister Bissoula's worktable, but Mme. Badoun was hard at work applying the wax. Now that President Bissoula had the gilded, hand-carved Louis XIV desk that stayed in the Presidential office, she had claimed its solid wooden counterpart from the Ministry offices. Mme. had directed the movers to place it with precision, and from behind the desk she could now see into the president's office, out the window to the gardens, and command both a view of the outer office door and the entrance to the inner chamber. The desk stood as an obstacle to all visitors; it was the gate, she the gatekeeper.

When Bissoula enlisted the support of former Ceremonial President Denis Sassou-Nguesso, the second round of the elections had become a formality. The result was a resounding victory for the former minister and professor; he had gathered 61% of the popular vote. Pascal Bissoula had become the first democratically elected head of state of the Republic of the Congo. The newspapers announcing this historic event, including *Le Monde,* were stacked on Mme. Badoun's desk, positioned to inform anyone who might be unmindful of Bissoula's landslide numbers.

Hearing a polite knock on the outer office door, Mme. Badoun looked up to see a tall, distinguished, and well-dressed man step quietly into the room. "Mme. Badoun?" he asked.

"Fareid Chamoun," he said. "I have an appointment with President Bissoula."

Mme. Badoun looked briefly at her appointment book and then back at Fareid, who stood patiently and respectfully awaiting further instructions. "You were not expected for another hour," she said.

"It is so," he replied, "but I was hopeful I might spend a few minutes with you in hopes you might provide the President more background information for my visit. I know that as a key advisor you have his trust and confidence, and possibly would be interested in providing him candid information to an early visitor," Fareid said. ". . . one who has been humbly referred to him by his dear friend, Thomas Kanza."

Mme. Badoun smiled and nodded once in acknowledgment, motioning Fareid to a chair next to her desk, "Please, Monsieur Chamoun."

Fareid took his place and deftly unbuttoned his suit coat, but remained sitting erect with hands politely folded in his lap, taking in the array of administrative and personal items covering Mme. Badoun's desk. In a matter of seconds, Fareid had gathered important pieces of intelligence that gave him a picture of the woman before him, her likes and dislikes, and her relationship with the new President. Other information he gleaned by absence. The lack of family photographs, for example, in spite of a conspicuous wedding band.

He knew how to proceed to the next step, but cautiously, very cautiously. *Once you were on the wrong side of Mme.,* he thought, *you would have permanently fallen from grace, with not the remotest chance of redemption.*

CHAPTER TEN

THE TARMAC AT Brazzaville's Maya-Maya airport was not much different in appearance from Abidjan's Houphouet-Boigny field. The uniformed guards wore the same camouflage and *de rigueur* aviator sunglasses. Ray Ban owes much to the military dictator Charles Taylor of Liberia, after whom most of the soldiers in sub-Saharan Africa fashioned their sense of intimidating appearance. The ubiquitous AK-47s were slung in similar fashion, loosely carried but magazine-ready, with extra clips in the belts of both men.

The Americans assembled at the base of the air stairs and again proceeded under the watchful eyes of the ramp guardians. Quinton kept an eye on Price, prepared to leap should his friend be overcome by an opportunity to capture a Moment on film. Price, aware he was being monitored, made several hand feints to the camera bag, appearing oblivious to Quinton's attentions. Professor Schmidt led the group forward, craning to see a familiar face, and Farber and Adrian brought up the rear of the column. The doors to the lower terminal opened on command to unveil the waiting crowd of well-wishers, families, supplicants, ne'er-do-wells, artisans, and persons interested simply in just being somewhere, any place where there was something going on.

Fareid Chamoun picked out Lake Schmidt first. He waved, smiling at Schmidt. Fareid stood well above most of the milling citizens, but bracketing him were two Congolese of equal stature. The two men in black suits and white shirts were cheerless and menacing, but ruggedly handsome, like aging boxers who had retired one bout short of a face-pulverizing end-of-career fight. They still possessed the ability to intimidate by presence alone. Were they to speak, the message would have been short and straightforward, but more likely would have involved merely a nod. Bissoula had sent them to greet the delegation and escort them to the hotel. Each now stood politely behind Fareid.

"Gentlemen! Gentlemen!" Fareid said in his familiar greeting. He embraced Schmidt, gave Quinton a two-handed grasp, and extended his hand to each of the group. "Welcome to the Congo!" he said to the gathered men, shaking each hand with enthusiasm. Farber noticed the two minders who stood motionless and almost invisible behind their sunglasses. Price and Adrian absorbed the scene with fascination, Adrian by now in full blink.

Their luggage loaded into two white Land Rovers, the group headed for the hotel. The driver of the first car pulled onto Maya-Maya Boulevard, heading south toward the river and the M'Bamou Palace. Schmidt, in the lead car's front passenger seat, turned to his friends in the back and pointed to a stadium off to their right.

"Curious, isn't it?" he said. "We are passing the Stade Massamba-Debat, a stadium named after the late President." Farber and Adrian ducked to look out the window at the passing building and grounds.

"Curious?" Adrian asked.

"Curious inasmuch as there appears to be no public grudge held against Monsieur Massamba-Debat. He was executed for involvement in the assassination of President Ngouabi, who's Museum is a mile or two east of here."

"De-Stalinization was expensive for the Soviets. Perhaps it was just a cost savings issue for the Congolese with Massamba-Debat," Farber noted.

Schmidt smiled, nodded, and looked at the driver. If he heard or understood the comments, the man behind the wheel gave no indication. His President was Pascal Bissoula, and his assignment was to deliver the Americans to the M'Bamou Palace hotel safely and quickly. He was grimly determined to do so.

As the two Rovers turned left onto the Avenue d'Omano, Schmidt pointed out the Palais de Justice de Brazzaville in the distance and said, "And the Palace of Justice stands about halfway between the Stadium named after the executed assassin and the Museum of the one he assassinated . . . ."

"Seems about right," Adrian said, cleaning his glasses with his tie.

Arriving at the front of the M'Bamou Palace Hotel, the delegation was greeted by a platoon of doormen and baggage handlers. The presence of the President's minders stirred a little extra hustle and interest from the hotel's front doorsmen.

"After check-in," Quinton said to the assembled men, "might I suggest we debrief in the rooftop bar?"

"Will this work, Maestro? Professor?" Quinton deferred to Fareid and Schmidt.

"Of course, my friend," Fareid said, "but be careful of the mosquitoes," referring to the HIV infected working girls. Rooftop bars, pool bars, and discotheques were swarming with young ladies whose trade had fallen dramatically due to the public awareness of the immune deficiency plague. Discounts for services were as rampant as the spread of the dread disease. One couldn't help but pity the girls who presented so beautifully in the evening, while moving one day closer to a horrible end the next.

The bar on the top floor of the hotel provided a grand view of the Congo River. Rich with nutrients and silt from upstream, the river was wide and swirling and murky. Huge rafts of greenery cut loose upriver floated seaward past the hotel. Men in pirogues, dugout canoes, plied their simple craft back and forth between Brazzaville and Kinshasa, carrying produce and the occasional passenger.

The skyline of Kinshasa, such as it was, could be seen easily from the Brazzaville shore, and the tallest building there had become an annoyance to past Brazzaville politicians and their friends at ELF Aquitaine. Not to be outbuilt by President Mobutu, a consortium had constructed the ELF Tower on the Brazzaville side of the river. It rose some 10 or 15 feet higher than the highest offering in Kinshasa. Not a big difference, but enough for those who measured.

The group had arrived singly and in pairs, and were finally all together at the chromed bar. Views of the river below and the passing parade on its surface held their attention until Fareid's "mosquitoes" began to alight on bar stools nearby.

"Someone keep an eye on Carey," Quinton said, fully understanding it would be he, himself, who would undertake the responsibility to keep Price's Christian duty under control.

"Yet, Daniel," Price said, "unarguably it's our Christian duty to be kind to God's creatures in peril."

"Precisely, my dear friend, and my kindness will be to protect one of God's creatures imperiled by his indiscriminate embrace of all humankind." Quinton looked at Price, and said for the benefit of all, "We have much to do without additional distractions, but I don't have to put too fine a point on that . . ."

Fareid nodded in agreement, then added, "President Bissoula has commitments for this evening, so he has had the hotel staff prepare a special meal for our first night."

To the delight and surprise of the group, waiters began filing into the bar area, where white tablecloths had been laid over joined tables to form a dining area. They carried plates heavy with fruits and salads garnished with purple cabbage leaves; steaming dishes of yellow rice, grilled red snapper and mounds of broiled shrimp followed.

Fareid led the procession into the secluded area and motioned for all to be seated. Chairs were pulled up to the table, plates began to be passed, wine glasses were topped off, and forks were poised for the dive, when Carey looked about, extended his hands, and said, "Would y'all . . . ?

"Could we just bow heads this time?" asked Quinton. Farber and Adrian nodded vigorously in support.

"Of course!" Price answered.

The waiters stood with hands folded and waited for the "Amen," which eventually arrived. More plates of unfamiliar fare appeared, were placed on the long table, and the feasting began in earnest. The evening had grown into night, and the lights of Kinshasa could be seen through the windows of the bar as reflections in the now dark river.

When the phone rang at two a.m., Quinton was in a deep well of sleep. The voice on the other end was husky.

"Daniel." Lake Schmidt said, "We've got a problem.

"Mark Adrian is having a severe reaction to something. I think it's the shrimp, although he said he's not allergic." Schmidt took a breath, "I mean to tell you, it's not pretty. His face is swollen and blotchy, and he says he wants to scratch his skin off."

Quinton sat up and turned the light on. "OK, partner. If you'll stay with Mark, I'll call the Embassy. Let's see if we can get him some help."

Quinton picked up the black dog-bone of a telephone and dialed the front desk. After many rings and a simple-but-direct request to ring the U.S. Embassy immediately, Quinton was connected to the Marine on duty.

"U.S. Embassy, Corporal Stanton," the voice said smartly.

"Morning, Corporal. Hate to call at this hour, but we have a medical emergency here at the M'Bamou Palace just down the road."

"Yes, sir. And who is this please?" the Corporal asked.

"Sorry. This is Daniel Quinton, Commander, U.S. Navy Retired, and I'm with an American delegation visiting at the request of President Bissoula." Quinton continued, "Ambassador Davidson is aware we're here, and we hope to be seeing him soon, but right now one of our party is having a bit of a medical emergency. Is there medical staff available at this hour?"

"Just a minute, Commander, let me check," and the phone clunked down on the desk at the other end.

Quinton wrestled with his pants and pullover shirt while he held the phone up to his ear with his right shoulder, then tried for his shoes, hopping around the bed on one foot within telephone cord's reach of the nightstand.

"Sir," the Corporal's voice interrupted Quinton's dance, "I'm afraid our Doc is on his rounds. He covers a lot of West Africa, and I think he's in Gabon this week."

"Understood. But our man needs to be seen tonight. Is there a local Doc you can send to the hotel?" Quinton urged.

"Yes, sir. My Sergeant said the Doc should be there in less than an hour," the Corporal replied.

"You're a good man, Corporal," Quinton said, and pushed the button in the cradle down to flash the operator.

"Lake," Quinton said when Schmidt picked up, "if you can get Mark dressed and down in the lobby, I'll meet you there. A doc's on the way and should be here in about half an hour or so."

"See you there," Schmidt said, and hung up.

CHAPTER ELEVEN

THE GIANT OIL company ELF Aquitaine, which casts a pervasive shadow over the Congo, traces its creation to General Charles de Gaulle, who in 1965, sought to create a national independence for France. There were two facets of the policy—one was military independence from its western allies, based on a national defense industry and supposed possession of a nuclear weapon; and the second, the independent control of the main sources of energy, uranium and oil.

ELF, an acronym for Essence Lubricants France, was assigned control of the oil, which was key to the continuing relations between France and most of her former colonies in Africa. Behind formal institutions, it worked through a system that political observers termed "international clientelism," wherein ELF combined force and corruption in economic, political, and public and private relations. In short, the company exerted power rivaling most nations.

The relationship between France and her recently independent African colonies was patrimonial, the patriarch caring for a son who has just come of age and been handed the keys to the car. The new governments might prosper, but only under the watchful eye of *Paris parentis*, and with the continuing flow of oil. ELF, through corruption and close association with the intelligence services, was to be used as a covert tool for maintaining the French presence in Africa. It was to be the pillar of Francafrique. More importantly for the Gaullists, ELF was to be the central financial source and monetary engine subsidizing their movement.

The organization of ELF was deliberately hazy. Networks overlapping networks created opportunities for deception and plausible deniability. These networks involved organizations and individuals which were both and often simultaneously public and private. Operating in this way, they blurred the boundaries between the government and those unrestrained by public protocol. Thus for ELF, its beneficiaries and African partners, corruption became a mode of governance.

CHAPTER TWELVE

I T SEEMED A long way from the M'Bamou Palace to the small stucco house where Laurent Ballieux was posted. He grumped to himself: *Nicer rooms at the hotel, and on top of that I have to share space with Fulbert DuLang.*

Ballieux viewed DuLang as one more Congolese he had to train to be a useful field agent, a task he felt was not imbued with even a distant chance of success.

Ballieux and DuLang had been sent from *Societé de Huile,* where DuLang was in training to be a field agent for the *Societé's* parent company, ELF Aquitaine. From Dulang's perspective, Ballieux would not have been his choice as a trainer either. He dressed inadequately, snored and displayed an array of repulsive personal habits. But choice was not a commodity among agents-in-training, so there they were in the living room of the four-room house on Avenue Amilcar Cabral awaiting a call from the "watcher" Ballieux had posted at the hotel. Ballieux dug absentmindedly into his right ear with a ballpoint pen. DuLang distracted himself from the senior agent's mining operation by reading the newspaper.

This was to be a simple surveillance operation and not much else. Ballieux, however, was hopeful of making more of it. He had discussed improving his chance for promotion with his handler, Georges Danou. "Just follow orders," Danou had advised. *Anyone can do that*, Ballieux thought, *but I will do more. I will come up with creatively aggressive ways to impress him.* The later it got, and the more empty wine bottles cluttered the floor, the more outlandish Ballieux's schemes became. But it was just the two of them, Ballieux and his trainee DuLang, and the brilliance of his tactics shone all the more brightly to Ballieux as the night wore on. It would become obvious to others when explained to them, he reasoned. And so it went, late into the evening.

The telephone on the end table next to Ballieux rang just after three a.m. He looked at DuLang, then picked up. "One of the Americans is very sick, and they have called the Embassy." Ballieux heard from the other end, then covered the receiver, and said to DuLang, "It is our watcher at the M'Bamou Palace. One of the Americans is ill."

"The American doctor is away, and they are sending a local one. So the hotel operator tells me," the watcher said into the phone, happily anticipating a bonus.

"*Merci,*" Ballieux said. "Stay there until I tell you different."

Ballieux hung up the phone. He looked at DuLang and said, "Dr. Fulbert DuLang, here is our chance."

DuLang stared blankly at his supervisor.

"We have castor beans!" Ballieux pointed to the garden.

Dulang's vacant expression didn't change.

"From castor beans come castor oil, but also from castor beans comes ricin," Ballieux explained. "If injected or inhaled, a bit of ricin the size of a pin head can kill you." Ballieux rose and began pacing the cramped living space. He nudged a wine bottle aside with his foot.

"In 1978, a Bulgarian dissident living in London, Georgi Markov, was poked with an umbrella tipped with ricin and died four days later. Had he not advised the hospital staff he had been pricked by a man who drove away in a cab, the doctors would not have discovered the ricin in his system. His death would have been a mystery. And we have castor beans here, right here!" Ballieux continued pacing, then paused near the stupefied DuLang.

"Of course, we do not need to kill the American, but we can make him violently ill, so sick he must leave the country. His compatriots will feel compelled to go with him. And if he dies, what does it matter. Go dress, my doctor-to-be, and I will make the castor bean solution."

Ballieux watched DuLang head for the bedroom, and said, "There will be a doctor's bag waiting for you at the hotel." He picked up the telephone, and listening for the dial tone, scanned the kitchen for a small container.

CHAPTER THIRTEEN

MARK ADRIAN, PRODIGIOUS consumer of shrimp and prawns, sat dejectedly in the hotel lobby of the M'Bamou Palace. His ardor for the local *fruits de mer* had been rewarded with a shocking display of reddening welts on his face and a crushing malaise. Adrian perched on the round seating area under the grand rotunda that commanded the lobby of the hotel. Schmidt and Quinton flanked the disconsolate man. The pair looked into the night outside the lobby windows for a sign of relief, while Adrian rocked gently and stared at the mural opposite.

The front doors of the lobby swung open in a gush, the ever-crisp doormen holding a bronze handle each, and through them blew a swirling arrangement of bright native dress, embroidered Nehru skull hat, and slippers curled up at the toe that moved toward the three Americans.

"Oh, my sainted mother!" Quinton said under his breath when he saw what he believed was the rescue doctor coming toward them. Mark Adrian sat up a little straighter, but kept his eyes on the tinted fresco on the arched ceiling across the lobby.

Quinton dared a look over Adrian's blotched-out head at his partner Schmidt. His eyes opened exaggeratedly wide with puzzlement, as he mouthed the word, "Doctor?"

Schmidt scowled at his friend, returning to watch the doctor's progress across the lobby. Adrian remained unblinking and groaned aloud, his face throbbing like a bass drum. The approaching gentleman wore thick glasses and a neck brace. He did have a medical bag, but the overall presentation worried Quinton. Adrian's stare was glued to the far wall.

"Good morning, gentlemen," the man said, placing his medical bag on the floor in front of Adrian. "I am Dr. Nguomo from World Health Organization. I was called by the Embassy."

Nguomo smiled to himself and opened the black bag on the floor. "I know what you're thinking . . . but I AM qualified. I believe Harvard Medical is still accredited, or at least it was when I graduated."

"When were you there?" Quinton asked.

Schmidt gave Quinton a look of disapproval. Quinton responded with a raising of his eyebrows, followed by an inquisitive shoulder shrug.

Dr. Nguomo, hand still in his open bag, fumbled with a syringe and vial. He moved awkwardly in his neck brace and adjusted his glasses, first looking over, then under the lenses. Quinton, watching the performance, gave Schmidt a look, mouthing the words, "What the . . . ?" Schmidt's eyes widened.

Dr. Nguomo's hand emerged from the bag bearing the vial and syringe. He then inexpertly drew the fluid into the needle, squirted, and tapped the syringe, as his lips pursed. He looked at Adrian with an air of confident patronage, as if to say, "Nothing to it, Old Sport."

Adrian in the meantime had been staring unrelentingly at the handpainted frescos on the lobby ceiling. The dazzling display of tropical flora and fauna, none of which were recognizable to Mark, somehow managed to calm him. Convinced this would be his last sight on the earthly plane, he had come to embrace the notion that one's last vision could be a hell of a lot worse than this. He fixed intently on a spider monkey.

The doctor reached for Adrian's right wrist and turned it to present the inside of his arm. He dabbed the appointed spot with an alcohol swab, injected the fluid, and finished with a swipe of the same swab.

Dr. Nguomo said, "There, that should help. You may not feel well for a while, but it will pass. Just rest quietly, my friend, even if there is a moment of extreme discomfort. This will be the corner you will turn. Then improvement will be yours."

The doctor pulled his bag together, patted Adrian's knee, and headed for the front doors. His pointed sandals made a slapping sound as he crossed the marble floor of the lobby. Reaching the entrance doors, Dr. Fulbert DuLang Nguomo spied the watcher. After a flicker of recognition, the doctor passed by the young man close enough to hand him a small fold of bills. He adjusted his brace once more, then moved off into the Brazzaville night.

"A marvel of modern science . . . and no goat entrails to decipher." Quinton muttered as he watched the doctor depart. "And you, Mark, will feel better almost immediately or die a horrible death, writhing in agony on the lobby floor in front of the guests and hotel staff, an embarrassment to your friends and countrymen. I will tell your family, however" he continued, "that you died bravely, having been hit with something more toxic than a day old street taco."

"Epinephrine rarely fails to put offending crustaceans in order, Mark," Schmidt informed Adrian. "I would ignore Not-a-Doctor Quinton's unfounded remarks." Schmidt glared at Quinton.

"Solid advice, Mark," Quinton said, "Feel any better?"

"Marginally better," Adrian said, as the pair of colleagues helped him toward the elevator. My head no longer feels like a blacksmith's anvil, just the horseshoe," Adrian said, gaining momentum. *When I get to the elevator*, he thought, *I'll be better still.*

"If it feels better to be the horseshoe, then you're gaining on it," Quinton said, looking over Adrian's head at Schmidt, eyes widened.

A white Land Rover pulled up to the *porte-cochère* fronting the M'Bamou Palace, and a young man wearing a dark suit and open-necked white shirt extracted himself from the rear seat. The driver stared straight ahead, as if unaware he was discharging a passenger. His chief concern was that the white Belgian doctor would not spend a lot of time at the hotel. On the SUV's door the Rod of Asclepius, a snake and stick, indicated the truck belonged to the United Nations, specifically, the World Health Organization. *Organisation Mondiale de la Santé* was scrolled across the lower section of the door below the initials W H O.

The discharged passenger, who was carrying a medical bag, walked toward the lobby door. Before he reached the first pillar of the overhanging façade, a man wearing khaki pants and a silk shirt with two low front pockets and an embroidered dragon accosted him. His untucked shirt hung loose, and the man had one hand posed in his lower left front shirt pocket, after the style of Charles, Prince of Wales.

"Are you Embassy Doctor?" asked the man with the dragon shirt.

"I have been contracted by the Embassy, yes," the doctor answered. "I am from World Health." He attempted to brush past the man, who represented the third or fourth annoyance of the day, three or four past the doctor's normal tolerance level.

Persistently blocking the doctor's path, the dragon-shirted man said, "Doctor! I have the good news to tell you of the American's much improvement." The doctor slowed, then stopped.

"Yes, the American is resting with quiet, after much exhaustion," the blocker said. "He sleeps in his room. He will be to call the Embassy *demain ou après-demain!*"

"And you are . . . ?" The doctor asked.

"I have the pleasure of employment at M'Bamou Palace, Monsieur Gonflé Bevue at your service."

But the doctor had already turned toward the small grove of palm trees where the Land Rover was parked. Over his shoulder, he said, "Tell your employers they will be billed," and headed for the SUV and the already napping driver slouched in the front seat.

Gonflé Bevue, the watcher, with another successful event to his credit, walked quickly into the hotel lobby to use the telephone. He was racking up a string of successes that would have to be compensated, and generously at that, he reasoned. Certainly better compensation than the insult of a gratuity passed to him at the front door by the medical imposter DuLang. He nodded briefly at the front desk clerk, picked up the telephone, and said into the receiver: "Outside line, s'*il vous-plait.*"

When Fulbert Dulang returned to the stucco house, he was still wearing the neck brace and the thick eyeglasses with the sturdy black frames. He checked himself in the car mirror, straightened his brace, picked up the medical bag from the back seat and headed for the front door. As he came through into the living room, DuLang could see Laurent Ballieux on the telephone. Ballieux's back was to the front door, and his left hand up to his ear, as if there were a bad connection.

Ballieux said, "Yes, yes, Gonflé, I can hear you." He turned while still holding the telephone and saw DuLang. His jaw dropped, but his mouth remained closed when he spied DuLang wearing his accoutrements.

Ballieux finished, "I will keep you advised of what I need, but tonight . . . well done!" He hung up the phone, staring at the black receiver a moment while he took a deep breath. Finally Ballieux looked up at DuLang and said, "Was this necessary?" motioning to the neck brace and glasses. Ballieux rubbed the bridge of his nose with his right thumb and forefinger.

"These are most effective methods. I learned this from no less a Spymaster than Ian Fleming himself." DuLang said

Ballieux shook his head, "You. You knew Ian Fleming."

"Well, no, but in his book," said DuLang, "I read about the neck brace. Maybe it was a movie. But no matter. 'No one wants to look too closely at the afflicted,' is what is known in the craft."

Ballieux stared in disbelief.

"And with these glasses, identifying me will be near the impossible!"

Ballieux motioned his colleague toward the couch, where they positioned themselves facing one another. DuLang still wore the brace.

"Tell me about the injection, and *mon Dieu*, take off that ridiculous necklace!"

Dulang unstrapped the brace, grudgingly placed his prop behind the couch, and then reached for the medical bag on the floor. He opened it, and stirred the contents, looking for the vial and syringe.

"Ow!" he said, drawing back quickly from the bag. "Ah, here it is." Dulang held up the syringe, handed it to Ballieux, then sucked on his fingertip where he had jabbed himself with the needle.

"And here is the vial." He handed it over to Ballieux, sitting back in the cushions.

Ballieux stared at the container. "This is Epinephrine." He looked at DuLang, waiting for a response. When none came, he asked, "Where is the castor bean solution?"

DuLang reached again for the bag and held the flaps open with both hands, peering into the darkness. He tilted the bag left, then right, the contents rattling around inside. "It is in here, somewhere. I only used a pin head's worth of the castor bean on the syringe . . . You said that much was deadly."

Ballieux looked incredulously at Dulang, and said, "A pin head of ricin poison, not the Castor bean solution."

"And if you put the solution on the syringe before you used the epinephrine vial, it will have no effect. No effect, at all." Ballieux slumped into the couch, muttering to himself, "A box of stones . . ."

CHAPTER FOURTEEN

T HE INVITATION TO dinner at the U.S. Ambassador's residence came as a surprise to Daniel Quinton and Lake Schmidt, but not to Fareid Chamoun. Checking in with the on duty officer at the Embassy, Schmidt had been modest in his description of the group, his chief aim being to inform the officials that the Americans were in country. In the event there was a problem during the stay, the Embassy would be able to react more quickly with the names of the visitors on record.

Fareid had loftier goals. Informing the duty officer was just the opener. He had procured a meeting with the Deputy Chief of Mission, Michael Harris, during his first visit and had informed the diplomat that he was principal advisor to the American Delegation.

"This is a distinguished group of gentlemen, sir, representing many facets of American commercial and political life," Fareid had told him. He continued, "Dr. Lake Schmidt is an eminent professor from Oxford, Cdr. Daniel Quinton has connections deep within the intelligence community, and the others are leaders in their fields. Steve Farber is a renowned litigator and author; Carey Price a recognized international financial and tax expert; and Mark Adrian has been involved with the largest hotel and resort developments of Prudential Group in Atlanta."

To Fareid, that Lake Schmidt was a professor from Oxford, Mississippi and not Oxford, England seemed a distinction not worth clarifying. The descriptors in the rest of the collective backgrounds seemed close enough.

Harris had been sitting back in his green leather chair. Had they been speaking by telephone, Fareid imagined, the polished brogans would have been propped on the desk in front of him. As Harris began to absorb the ever-so-mildly bloated resumes of the group, he moved closer to the desk top, unclipping a Mont Blanc fountain pen from his shirt pocket.

"My apologies, Mr. Chamoun, please tell me the names of the gentlemen again and, if you would be so kind," Harris added, feigning interest, "spell first and last names." Fareid waited until Harris had carefully adjusted his French cuffs, checked the operation of his ink pen, and lightly and precisely rested his forearms on the desk in front of him.

Harris looked at Fareid over the top of his tortoise shell spectacles and said, "Go ahead."

After Harris had carefully scribed the names, finishing with a dash and a dot, Fareid continued, "My partners, Schmidt and Quinton, are the movers of the delegation, and I am responsible for the meeting with President Bissoula. So should Ambassador Davidson feel inclined to establish an excellent working relationship with our team—a team positioned to provide intelligence of the first order—we would be delighted to accept an invitation to dinner at the residence."

Harris straightened in his chair, taking a fresh look at the man opposite him. Fareid sat relaxed in his chair, hands folded politely in his lap, but his polar-ice blue eyes stared, unblinking, intimidating, unsettling at best. Harris found himself fumbling with his leather desk blotter and the papers arranged on it. He was unable to look at Fareid straight on, but said, "Yes, Mr. Chamoun, an excellent idea. I will check the Ambassador's schedule and consult the Protocol Officer."

Harris stood and offered his hand across the desk, summoning the courage to glance quickly at Fareid, who smiled, bowed slightly, then turned toward the door.

"We are at the M'Bamou Palace as guests of his Excellency, the President. One of our delegation checks the front desk for messages frequently. We may be contacted there.

"It has been a pleasure, Monsieur Harris." Fareid left, closing the door behind him.

CHAPTER FIFTEEN

THE EVENING THE delegation was invited to dinner at the Ambassador's residence was warm and humid and still. A bitten-sugar-cookie of a moon rose in the night sky and hung over the lights of Kinshasa to the south. White stucco buildings on the grounds of Ambassador Davidson's home reflected the moonlight on high walls that stretched above bougainvillea and elephant ear clustered below. An air conditioning unit droned behind the front wall. Several civilian guards paced casually around the perimeter of the residence, moving silently in and out of shadow. They wore dark open shirt-jackets with dark trousers, and would stop and talk quietly with one another where the wall turned and ran back toward the river. The men were barely visible, until one of them would draw on a cigarette and the small ember could be seen through the foliage.

Fareid Chamoun reached the front gate first, followed closely by Lake Schmidt, then Daniel Quinton. Other guests were inside the courtyard and could be heard being greeted by Mrs. Davidson. Piano music drifted through the open front door along with the inviting sound of ice being dropped into cocktail glasses. The exotic aroma of local fare roasting on open grills filled the night air. The social machinery of the

U.S. Foreign Service in Brazzaville, Congo was building up a head of steam.

"You must be Fareid Chamoun and the American Delegation," Mrs. Davidson said, greeting the three men as they stepped up onto the flagstone terrace that led to the residence.

"Madam," Fareid said, bowing slightly, "I have the pleasure to introduce Dr. Lake Schmidt, and Cdr. Daniel Quinton, my friends and partners."

Schmidt and Quinton shook hands with Mrs. Davidson and were ushered into the foyer by a well turned out black man in a white serving jacket, his graying hair combed straight back. Broad, carpeted steps led up to the main living area, where Ambassador Davidson held his Russian counterpart by the forearm and spoke quietly. The brown-suited Russian diplomat nodded in agreement with his host, but looked up when the three men entered the living space, which alerted the Ambassador.

"Good evening, gentlemen," Davidson said, turning to greet the group. "Thank you for joining us. May I introduce you to my friend, Alexei Yurasov, Ambassador from the Russian Republic."

Yurasov greeted each of the Americans with an unblinking stare and the slightest of smiles. His hair was short-cropped, and he had the look of a reconstructed wrestler. His round head was decorated with calluses and scar tissue from personal confrontations in the ring, or, more likely, in poorly-lit places while re-enlightening recalcitrant comrades who had strayed from the path.

But that was all in the past, thought Schmidt. *KGB or GRU*, thought Quinton, who watched as Fareid took Yurasov's hand with a respectful bow.

"Excellency . . . Fareid Chamoun. So nice to meet you," he said.

———

"Pleasure, Mr. Ambassador," Quinton nodded, meeting the Russian's stare with one of his own.

Sensing the tension, Schmidt interjected quickly, "Excellency, Dr. Lake Schmidt. It is an honor."

The Russian opened his arms to all, turning slightly to keep Quinton in his fore vision, and said, "Ambassador Davidson again has brought an interesting group of dinner guests together, agree? Yet, I don't see your other colleagues, Mr. Farber, Mr. Price, and uh, Mr. Adrian. How is he feeling, Dr. Schmidt?"

Quinton and Schmidt looked at Yurasov, then at the cocktails they'd been handed by a silently-gliding small black man. Quinton, answering for Schmidt, said, "Evidently you heard he was not well. Might I ask how you came by that information, Mr. Ambassador?"

Yurasov looked at Davidson, then at Schmidt, who was shifting his feet uncomfortably, and addressed Quinton. "It is a small village, Brazzaville, yes? Your presence here is known among the small circle of internationalists, Mr. Quinton. Of course, the M'Bamou Palace is center for visitors of distinction, particularly guests of President Bissoula, and activities there are much scrutinized. I hope you take no offence by my question. I assure you it was out of courtesy."

Schmidt glared at Quinton, and replied, "Mr. Ambassador, no offense taken. Old ways die hard with my partner."

"Some ways never do," Yurasov smiled at Quinton.

"Indeed." Schmidt said. "But to answer your kind inquiry, Mr. Adrian is quickly improving. He will be avoiding the *Capitaine Grille* seafood selection in future. Our colleagues Farber and Price have stayed with him to monitor his recovery. Doctor Nguomo treated him with epinephrine I believe, and it had an immediate beneficial effect."

"At first we were a bit jarred by his appearance, with the pointed Arabian-looking slippers and African robes, but it was the neck brace and thick glasses rounding out the outfit that got us wondering where the gentleman came from," Quinton joined in.

Fareid had stopped in mid-sentence with Mrs. Davidson when the Ambassador and Quinton became engaged in conversation, but on hearing the description of the doctor who attended Adrian, he excused himself from the group encircling the Ambassador's wife and worked toward the group standing with the Russian Ambassador. Arriving at Quinton's side, he gently took his arm and steered him aside, asking, "Was the doctor an African, a black African?"

"Yes he was, Fareid. Why do you ask? Is there something we need to be worried about?" asked Quinton.

Fareid raised his hand and extended his forefinger. "One minute," then continued with his questioning: "Would you recognize him again if you met face to face? What did you say he was wearing?"

"Some folded shirt and cloak arrangement of African design, and pointed Arabian slippers." Quinton said. "And I believe I would recognize him, in spite of the neck brace and thick glasses; glasses he didn't appear to need."

Fareid said, more to himself, "Neck brace . . ."

"Is Mark in jeopardy here?" Quinton asked, trying to gauge a reaction from Fareid.

"No, my friend, not now. If he is improving after last night, he will recover. But we must be very cautious whom we deal with on every level. You and my professor must keep me advised of all contacts, yours and our friends back at the hotel, our Innocents Abroad." Fareid scanned the room, looking for Schmidt. "There are serious people who do not wish us well in our undertakings. Not only will they throw a banana skin in our path, but worse."

"Understood," Quinton said, and followed Fareid toward the dining room, where the other guests were being guided to their seats.

The Ambassador's residence sat high on a bluff overlooking the Congo River, and at night the lights of Kinshasa spread across the river like an expanding galaxy. The central space of the residence, with its spectacular view, was dominated by a competition-size pocket billiard table. From every position in the room and around the pool table, the night sky and river were on display. On the wall opposite the river, a long mahogany bar ran the length of the room and turned for several feet against the adjoining wall. Shelves behind the bar ran to the ceiling and were solidly packed with books, wines, liqueurs, and a 1200-count cigar humidor, which anchored the middle section. The post of Ambassador to the Congo had been filled exclusively by men from the first posting year in 1960, and the furnishings of the residence reflected the tastes of those occupants, formally titled Ambassador Extraordinary and Plenipotentiary, a designation intended to impress.

If not by the title, Schmidt and Quinton were impressed when they were invited by the Ambassador to join him and Yurasov in a game of eight ball in the "Billiards Room" after dinner. The gray-haired manservant appeared once again without advertisement, and offered the Americans a selection and their choice of cigars, none of which had wrappers. Quinton selected a snifter and a cigar, rolling it between his fingers while looking at the Russian Ambassador.

"Cuban, of course," Yurasov said.

Davidson nodded toward his friend, "Illegal for us to import, certainly, but not to smoke." He motioned for his gray-haired domestic to cut the guests' cigars.

Quinton handed his cigar over, saying, "Cut me, Mick." Then "Shall we lag for break?" disappointed no one appeared to appreciate his reference to Burgess Meredith's character in the movie "Rocky."

As Yurasov stood over his first shot, Davidson moved toward the Americans and said, "Your endeavors to bring new trading partners to the Congo, particularly Western trading partners, are of much interest to the State Department. It would most assuredly be of interest to Bissoula. Particularly if there are concessions that would help fill Presidential coffers. He is desperate for funds to cover his return to governance, and, as are all African heads of state, desperate for funds to stay in power."

Davidson moved to the table rail, picked up a chalk to dress his cue stick, and continued, "As a word of caution, and just among us lads, be very cautious when speaking to and around Mme. Moulon-Badoun. She is a force in Bissoula's world. She controls appointments, screens visitors, offers counsel, and it is widely known though seldom mentioned, she provides a wide range of informal aid and comfort to the Head of State. All this, of course, confers great power and leverage upon the President's secretary."

Fareid, mingling with the other guests in the living room, kept an eye toward the Billiards Room. When Ambassador Davidson moved around the table toward his partners, he disengaged himself and headed for the group of men talking together and watching Yurasov line up his next shot.

"The best source for revenue for Bissoula, of course, also happens to be the jugular vein for France—oil concessions. Concessions jealously protected by ELF Aquitaine," Davidson concluded.

Fareid stepped quickly up the landing and slipped into the group. "Gentlemen," he said. "I couldn't help but overhear you mention the force of evil, ELF Aquitaine."

"The Ambassador was telling us of the President's need for financial help to shore up his administration, and that oil concessions were his trump card," Schmidt said. "And ELF, of course, holds that these concessions are their exclusive preserve and that of their homeland."

"Perhaps," said Fareid, "but there are other projects and enterprises our team can bring to the President without crossing the path of ELF. Our intention is not to disturb the viper, rather to build partnerships in the West, the U.S. most importantly, that will allow Bissoula and his country to dig out of their economic hole and prosper. An economic hole, I believe, created by the oil slick controlled by Paris."

"In other words, Paris and her dark agent, ELF Aquitaine" Quinton concluded.

"You will forgive me, Mr. Chamoun, but my staff advises me you may have continuing interests in Occidental Petroleum in Dallas," interjected Davidson, watching for Fareid's reaction. "Of course, you understand background has been gathered on all guests invited to the Residence, a formality with which I'm sure you are acquainted. But I mention Occidental so we all might understand how 'the viper,' as you call ELF, will view your being here. Were they not in the mix in the Congo, it would be a very boring posting indeed."

Fareid looked at the Ambassador, then at his colleagues, and said, "Sir, our delegation is not here to compete with ELF for oil leases. We represent many sectors of the commercial market, and petroleum is not one."

"As you say, Mr. Chamoun, but I assure you ELF has access to the same information concerning your association, or should I say former association, with Walid Hammoud, and I would expect them to be troubled. In spite of your protestations, they will be watching the activities of you and your group. Watching with interest." Davidson motioned Quinton toward the table, and said, "I believe it is your shot, Commander."

Schmidt and Quinton stood by the window, finishing their drinks, Quinton savoring the last of his cigar. "What do you think about the Occidental thing, Lake?"

"Not entirely sure, Daniel. Fareid has always been very close hold about Hammoud and the Occidental connection. May be oil leases are not in his crosshairs, but in any case, we don't want QSCI to get involved in the 'erl bidness,' as they say in Texas. Kanza's concerns about that industry are well founded. I don't know about Fareid. He says Oxy is not a topic he will discuss. I thought because of Hammoud, but I'm not absolutely certain he has made a clean break with that side of the family. We must ask him straight out if he contemplates the unthinkable, competing with ELF for concessions that will be sold to Oxy."

"I agree," Quinton said. "Besides, partner, don't want anything to detract from this evening. This is one of those that stays as a clear image for a long time."

Quinton paused and took a pull on his cigar, looking up, then down river. "Fix this moment in your mind Herr Dr. Schmidt. We are looking out over the Congo River from the American Ambassador's residence on a starlit night, drinking his Armagnac, smoking someone's private stock of Cuban cigars, and kicking the Russian Ambassador's ass in eight ball." Quinton surveyed the room, "Further proof God loves us and wants the West to triumph."

'Hard to argue that tonight, partner," Schmidt said in agreement. "Hard indeed."

Quinton frowned, "But I do agree, Lake, we want nothing to do with a running gun battle with ELF. For that, we are painfully outmatched."

Fareid had been watching the two and joined them at the window. Davidson and Yurasov were taking their time re-racking the billiard balls, Davidson scanning the room, seeking another tray of snifters being circulated by The Small Gray One.

"My friends, it has been a delightful evening, but perhaps we should return to the hotel now and compare our perceptions while they are fresh," Fareid said quietly. "We should pay our respects to the Ambassador and Madame, His Excellency Comrade Yurasov and the other guests." He strode off in the direction of Mrs. Davidson, and the pair followed.

At the front terrace, Ambassador Davidson stood bidding goodnight to the departing guests, and when Schmidt and Quinton crossed the threshold into the now cool evening, Davidson said, "Please keep me advised of any difficulties you run into, particularly if it appears ELF or the French may be involved. Americans are not their favorite tart on the dessert tray. The French never forgave us, you know, for saving them time and again. And keep an eye on your Lebanese partner. I mean that in the sense of keeping him out of harm's way. Fearlessness is not always a virtue."

Schmidt nodded, saying, "We will indeed. Thank you for a fine evening." Quinton agreed, then added, "And thank you for being the gracious host, letting Dr. Schmidt and me prevail at the billiard table."

"Not at all, gentlemen, I was trying my damnedest to win. I'll need to upgrade my partner," Davidson smiled, looking back at an inebriated and weaving Yurasov who was leaning in toward a backing-away Mrs. Davidson. "Billiards partner, that is," he amended, and turned back inside to rescue his beleaguered spouse.

CHAPTER SIXTEEN

HE TWO WHITE Land Rovers were parked outside the hotel
lobby entrance next to a row of palm trees, each captured in a
giant terra cotta urn. One of the drivers had hiked his foot up on the
front bumper of the lead car and was smoking a cigarette. The other
driver had rolled all his windows down, cocked his head back on the
driver's headrest, and, his mouth agape, was in full slumber. They had
been waiting for the American delegation for over an hour.

Lake Schmidt appeared first. He moved toward the front entrance
and looked to see if Bissoula's men were out front. Spotting the white
SUVs, he motioned to the rest of the group. The men were conservatively
dressed in lightweight dark suits and white shirts with variations on a red
tie. Carey Price was the exception, sporting a "Matlock" blue seersucker
suit and a South Carolina Fighting Gamecocks bowtie. Buffed up white
bucks completed the Southern ensemble, worn with quiet confidence by
the tax lawyer.

When the group joined Schmidt, he reminded them of the protocol
concerning President Bissoula's receptionist, Mme. Badoun. "This will
be a fascinating, and it is hoped, mutually beneficial meeting with the
President. Remember, though, as Fareid has instructed, leave even the

most inconsequential conversation with Badoun to him. Silence and respect are the watchwords in the presence of the good Madame." The men all nodded in agreement.

Fareid was running late as usual, so asked Lake and Quinton to take the group on ahead with Bissoula's drivers. "I have transport, my friend, and will join you shortly," he advised Schmidt. "There is some behind the scenes work to do. Work that will condition the atmosphere."

The Land Rovers pulled away from the hotel and headed west on Avenue Simon Kimbangou. From the front seat of the lead vehicle, Schmidt watched the passing pedestrians trodding earnestly toward their destinations, many carrying parcels on motionless heads. Their pace was slow but deliberate, some walking miles from market to deliver simple everyday provender to even simpler homes.

In the back seat behind Schmidt, Quinton had been watching the same transient parade. "Life seems to be passing by at an acceptable tempo for the men and women in the street. Not a fancy life, but quiet and peaceful it appears." Turning to look at the road behind them, he could see the Land Rover following, but no sign of Fareid.

The two-vehicle caravan slowed and came to a stop at the intersection where Avenue Kimbangou joins Avenue de Djoue. In the left turn lane, next to the lead Land Rover, a green field jeep with the doors removed sat idling, steaming in the heat of the asphalt road. The front seat passenger wore a faded khaki bush jacket, and he moved his right hand up to adjust the temple of his sunglasses. Between the man and the side of the jeep frame, the wooden pistol butt of a shortened pump shotgun protruded, and the man's hand came down from his face to rest lightly on the grip.

The movement immediately caught Quinton's eye, and he screamed at the driver, "Shooter! GO! GO!" Schmidt turned and saw the shotgun being drawn from the jeep and yelled, "Keep going!" to the startled driver.

The blast came fast and loud, ripping through the rear quarter panel of the Rover. The next shot, seconds later, was just as loud as the first but failed to strike the now accelerating SUV. A woman on the sidewalk carrying a basket of food watched in amazement, then took the force of the expanding pellets of the second round full in the chest. Her basket and its contents flew into the air in an eruption of vegetables and basket fragments. Nearby walkers screamed and rushed to help the fallen woman. The jeep had backed and rammed into the car behind it, squealed into a U-turn, hopped the median, and headed in the opposite direction down the Avenue.

Quinton rolled down his window and motioned with his right arm for the following Rover to speed up and stay with the lead. Schmidt was yelling now, "We have to go back! We have to go back!" The driver, bug-eyed and confused, looked at the pair. Quinton shouted to him "Move! Keep moving!" The driver returned his attention to accelerating down Avenue de Djoue toward the Palais de Justice, his hands vise-gripped to the steering wheel.

Quinton turned to his partner and shouted above the rattling of the fast moving Rover, "Lake, nothing we can do back there! That may not be the only shooter; we gotta keep going!"

He looked behind them, and saw that the driver of the other SUV was closing the gap. Quinton could see Adrian in the front seat, holding on to the door strap, eyes opened wide, very wide. Price had pulled himself up between the front seats and was encouraging the driver to stay close. Farber had turned in the rear seat to see what he could out the back window. "The woman is down! My God!"

"Where's the jeep! Is it behind us? Where is it? Where is it?" Price shouted, looking left, then up and down the boulevard.

"No! It's over the median and going the other way!" Farber shouted back. "Mark, are you OK?" he added grasping Adrian by the shoulder.

"What the hell . . ." Adrian said.

"Mark! Are you OK?" Farber asked again.

"What the hell . . ." Adrian said, and stared straight ahead at the speeding Rover headed for the meeting with the President.

CHAPTER SEVENTEEN

THE CHILDREN PLAYING soccer in the front yard of the small stucco house scattered when the field jeep slid to a halt in the gravel and red sand space adjacent to the street. Two men exited, one sweating and swearing, as he lugged a wrapped package and two black pouches toward the house. The taller man, in a khaki bush jacket, was berating his companion. It appeared he was on the verge of taking a swipe at him. Once, he raised the package as if to bludgeon the smaller man, who was now scuttling toward the house.

A honey-colored mongrel dog belonging to one of the fleeing soccer players barked at the pair. Tied to the front porch post, she was unsure why she had been left behind.

Ballieux unwrapped the shotgun and said to DuLang, "Get that bitch out of here."

DuLang reached down and cut the cord restraining the frightened animal. She ran toward an opening in the fence, and Ballieux raised the gun and fired off a round just as DuLang screamed, "No!"

The blast caught the fleeing dog in her hind legs and threw her up against the fence wire. Unable to run on all fours, she pulled herself up on front legs and dragged through the hole in the fence, yelping in pain. DuLang looked on helplessly. In the distance, behind a low concrete block wall, he could see one of the young boys who had been playing soccer in the yard holding a small girl, probably his sister, who was crying uncontrollably as she watched the scene unfold.

Ballieux rewrapped the shotgun and headed for the house. The screen door slammed, and the front door closed behind it with a bang as Ballieux pushed DuLang into the house. The lock rammed home, and the venetian blind in the small window at the top of the door came down in a clatter. Tattered drapes framing the front windows of the house closed in a whoosh; first one, then the other.

"What were you doing with that driving?" Laurent Ballieux screamed at Fulbert DuLang, who stood in the middle of the room with slouched shoulders supporting a bowed head and a dejected face. "You were supposed to wait for the second shot, then leave room to maneuver, to escape without crashing with another car! You are a moron, incompetent beyond the imagination!"

DuLang, still shaken but recovering, pulled himself up straight, and said, "And you, Ballieux the genius, killed an innocent woman on the street, missing the Americans. Now we are deep in the *merde*!" He inched backward as Ballieux raised the mare's leg of a shotgun that had come fully unwrapped once they were inside the house.

"I won't hit you, stupid one" Ballieux said, stepping a pace closer to DuLang. The butt of the shotgun swung up with lightening speed and caught DuLang below the jaw before he could make the slightest move. The crack of the wooden stock against bone was loud, and Dulang went down. *I should have expected that,* Dulang thought in a haze, the pain welling up in his head. He fought hard to focus on the wooden grain of the floorboard to keep from passing out. He had lifted himself on his hands and knees when Balluiex's foot found his rib cage with a vicious kick that partially raised him off the floor. All of the air went out of DuLang, and he felt himself propelled to the floor by a powerful shove from Balluiex's other foot. DuLang lay still, unable to do much but wait for the *coup de grace*, which he believed was inevitable and about to occur in the next few seconds.

"Get up Idiot," Ballieux commanded.

DuLang moaned and tried to move. He felt Ballieux grab his shirt collar and belt, felt himself being hoisted into the air, and set standing, wobbly and dazed, in front of the bigger man.

"You do not follow instructions, you pile of dung!"

Ballieux, breathing hard, was inches from DuLang's face. On top of the beating he had just received, DuLang was further assaulted by Ballieux's tobacco-sweat-and-garlic stench. "Because you reversed, I had no choice but to shoot the woman. I wanted to splatter blood, but it should have been American."

"Who was she?" DuLang whispered.

"I don't know. No reason to care. I merely saved her from a miserable life." Ballieux grabbed DuLang by the shoulders, then said, "My friend," and kissed him on the forehead. Stunned first from the beating, then the reversal of treatment, DuLang was standing with his mouth agape when the open right hand of Ballieux came crashing across his face.

"Follow instructions, *mon ami*, and all will be well." Ballieux steadied DuLang and made a pretense of brushing the dust off the smaller man's lapels. He patted the beaten man on the cheek and said, "We must return to work. Now we will eliminate that big slab of Lebanese meat, Chamoun!"

CHAPTER EIGHTEEN

THE SOLDIERS IN the courtyard at the Palais de Justice could see the two Land Rovers lurching around the traffic circle near the *Centre Culturel Français* as they sped toward the Presidential offices. White dry dust and gravel kicked up behind the pair of SUVs could be seen blocks away by the Presidential attendants. One of the soldiers ran toward the guard shack to call the Corporal of the Guard. The soldier in the shack was already notifying Bissoula's office that the American's were arriving sooner than expected and seemed in a bit of a rush.

From the window of the second floor Bissoula and Fareid Chamoun watched the approaching caravan. A third car with flashing lights and a yodeling siren had joined the Rovers. The cars came to a skidding halt in the stone-strewn courtyard, and a Brazzaville police officer clambered from his cruiser, running up to first one SUV, then the other. Bissoula and Fareid could hear him ask, "All right? Everyone all right?"

Fareid watched his friends extract themselves from the vehicles, and said, "Excellency, there has been a problem for my colleagues. I am not certain, but I suspect ELF is involved, directly or otherwise. I must see to them now."

Fareid bowed modestly toward Bissoula, adding, "Sir, my friends know nothing of our discussions and will be surprised I am here ahead of them. What we have spoken of today must be kept in the strictest confidence. With your kind permission, I will attend to my friends."

Bissoula nodded, then said, "If you turn right down the hallway, there will be a set of stairs on your left. Take them and you will be outside in the rear courtyard. You may join your friends after they are in the first reception area. They will not know I have seen you in my private quarters. *Bon chance*."

Fareid moved quickly toward the door and slipped quietly down the hallway.

The group of Americans shuttled hurriedly toward the side door a few yards to the right of the main entrance. Two soldiers and the police officer ran with them, looking right, left, and up toward the rooftop for any sign of hostility. Three guards remained in the courtyard, facing the entrance and the outer walls, AK-47s unslung. The door closed with a slam after the Americans were inside. On cue from the Corporal of the Guard, the police officer remained outside and took position astride the entrance.

Inside the reception area, other petitioners stared in surprise at the dusty and ruffled group of men who had just blown through the side door. One of the soldiers stayed with them, while the Corporal headed for the door leading to the inner reception area. Knocking lightly, he holstered his weapon and opened the door. A man in a dark suit greeted him, and pointed toward the center of the room. He looked briefly at the Americans, then shut the door softly.

"Never did like a flashy entrance," Quinton said to Schmidt, "but there you have it." He turned to the others and saw they were leaning in to check on Adrian. Quinton asked, "Mark, how're you doing?"

"What the hell just happened?" Adrian struggled to remember when he was last in control of his surroundings. It seemed months ago.

The men pulled chairs from the wall into a semi-circle and tended to Adrian, who was still suffering from his dining and medical experience at the hotel. Steve Farber remained standing, then started to pace. "That must have been a mistake. Why would we be targets for anybody? Surely that shooting was not aimed at us." Price looked at Farber and shrugged. "Steve, we stick out here like Mormon missionaries at a strip club. How could we possibly be mistaken for some other group?"

"You're right, my friend." Quinton said, "They were after us."

The side door through which the group had burst flung open again, and there stood Fareid, filling the doorway with his large frame, genuine concern, and growing bewilderment.

"What has happened? My friends, what has happened?" He moved toward the huddled group, assessing Schmidt, hopeful he among the men would be able to recount the events accurately and without hysteria.

Schmidt stood, and motioned to Fareid with outspread arms to represent the rest of the group. "We were attacked, Fareid. We are all OK, but I think a woman was killed by mistake. It all happened so fast."

Fareid was now genuinely bewildered: "What?" He looked at the group with renewed concern, then looked at Quinton, "Daniel?"

"A field jeep, two men, a driver and a shooter, Fareid. Shooter: right handed, sawed-off 12 gauge pump." Quinton looked at the others and continued, "Front seat passenger fired into our Rover, we were in the lead. We were stopped when it happened—so was he—not a hard shot if he meant to kill one of us. We took some buckshot in the left rear quarter panel. That's all."

Quinton could see Fareid was assessing the rest of the delegation, particularly Adrian, but he continued. "The driver reversed just as the shooter was pumping out another shot, and a woman on the sidewalk took the full blast. Don't think she made it."

The others nodded in agreement. Farber said, "We didn't get a good look, Fareid. Carey and I were in the rear seat and only saw the jeep crashing into the car behind. We saw the woman go down, and then the jeep was gone."

Price added, "That poor woman. Why, in heaven's name, would this happen? Who would do this?" He looked at Adrian, and Fareid followed his eyes, seeing that Mark had not yet recovered from the episode. Fareid shook his head slowly and said, "My God, this cannot be." He turned to Quinton. "Did you recognize either of the men in the jeep? Anything strike you as familiar?"

Quinton looked at Schmidt, and said, "The shooter was big, unshaven, and appeared European. Never seen him before. The driver, though, looked familiar, but I'm not sure why."

"What was familiar to you, Daniel? His face, his size, his mannerisms . . . dress?" Fareid peered intently at Quinton, hoping to focus his memory on any detail of the event.

Quinton looked at Schmidt, then Adrian, then said, "Did either of you see any resemblance to Dr. Nguomo, that doctor at the hotel? Don't know why that strikes me. I just got a quick glimpse."

"Maybe, had he been wearing a neck brace and thick glasses," Schmidt said, "but he had neither."

Adrian slumped farther down into the chair and said quietly, "It was loud, very loud."

"Do you think that's possible, Fareid, that there's a connection?" Quinton asked.

"I do not know my friend, but it is not for us to resolve. The authorities will investigate and find out—*maybe* find out who it was—and why it happened. In the meantime, we must meet with the President and carry on with our endeavors. All willing and agreed?" The group nodded in unison. Fareid added, "I believe the President will be distressed we have met with such violence. Until the attackers are apprehended, I will ask him for protection, at the hotel and while driving. He will agree, I am confident." Fareid looked again at Adrian, and said, "We will be fine; no one can touch us."

The transition from linoleum-floored waiting area to President's antechamber was dramatic in style, presence and temperature. Several window air conditioners hummed pleasantly, and light yellow carpet stretched to full drapes hanging across the walls opposite and adjoining the President's door. Commanding the room was the desk of Mme. Badoun. And commanding the desk and all that came into view was Madame herself.

Her eyes went straight to Fareid. "His Excellency will be just a few minutes, but looks forward *avec plaisir* to meeting with the delegation."

"*Merci*, Madame. May I introduce you to the group?" This pleased Mme. Badoun, but she remained behind her desk, standing as the men were introduced one by one.

As the delegation filed into the President's office, Mme. Badoun touched Fareid on the arm and said, just loud enough so all of the men could hear, "Monsieur Chamoun, would you please be so kind to sign the registry for your delegation?" Quinton and Schmidt shared a glance as they moved with the group into the office and the door closed part way.

"Madame?" Fareid said to the now-seated woman.

"We have no registry, Fareid, that has already been attended to. I wanted to tell you of someone you might want to contact about the ugliness of today toward your friends."

Fareid turned slightly to check the door to the President's office, and turned back to Mme. Badoun.

"My cousin knows a man, Gonflé Bevue, who is working at the M'Bamou Palace as a watcher for ELF. I believe Bevue is watching you and your friends." Badoun peeked at the partially open door, then motioned to Fareid, shooing him along with a quick backhanded brush: "Go, the President is waiting! Bevue wears a dragon shirt," she whispered as Fareid turned toward the door.

Tall and solidly built, the former botany professor, Marxist-Socialist activist, and Minister of Agriculture, now stood as the first democratically elected President of Congo-Brazzaville. Pascal Bissoula had welcomed each of the Americans with a warm handshake and asked them to be seated in the gilded chairs drawn up around the large semi-circular desk.

"I want you to create economic opportunities in Congo for investors in the U.S. and throughout the West. These opportunities, of course, will lead to jobs for my countrymen." Bissoula continued, "A life is fulfilled and happy only when it is based in meaningful work for the individual. We must show my people that this environment, an environment where there is unlimited opportunity, is best created in a framework of democratic governance, *n'est ce pas?*

"But there is a secondary component to your mission, should we agree to enter into a relationship. And that is to burnish the reputation of Congo in America and all the capitals of Europe. This of course not only goes hand in glove with encouraging investment in West Africa, but also restores our standing at the United Nations, the World Bank, and the International Monetary Fund. We must find the resources, for we have the political will." Bissoula sat down, and Fareid stood, motioning to the others that the meeting had come to an end. Hesitantly, they all stood, surprised at the brevity of the encounter.

As the group moved toward the door and began filing out, Bissoula looked at Fareid and raised his forefinger. As Schmidt, Quinton and the others gathered in the reception office. Fareid said, "I will be just one minute, one minute," and closed the door to the President's office.

"As you know, Fareid, ELF is very important to French national interests, and we must tread very lightly in matters which concern them most," Bissoula said.

"Yes, Papa," Fareid said. Bissoula smiled at the familiar but deferential phrase.

"Bring the resources, my Lebanese son," Bissoula held his fatherly smile, but then turned deadly serious: "Do not delay, Fareid Chamoun. It is a matter of survival. Do what you need to do to bring Occidental."

"I will, Excellency, I assure you, I will." Then, "Today in the streets? I know ELF was involved in what happened," Fareid said. "Violence to innocents is abhorrent to me. And my friends, Excellency, are innocents."

"As was the poor woman on her way home from market," Bissoula reminded him.

"It is so . . . all the more reason to hunt down these criminals. But, I beg you, Mr. President, help keep my colleagues safe during our stay here." Fareid glanced toward the door and moved closer to Bissoula: "I know your security forces will do their best to protect my group and apprehend the killers. And on my part, I will make every effort to bring them to justice."

"Yes, justice. But justice administered at the *Palais de Justice*," Bissoula admonished, staring unflinchingly at Fareid.

The big man took a small step back, made a slight bow, and said, "God willing," then let himself out of the Presidential office.

CHAPTER NINETEEN

THE DELEGATION DROVE in silence back to the hotel. The Land Rovers came to a stop in front of the lobby and were quickly approached by two men who came through the front doors. They were dressed casually. Khaki slacks and shirts open-collared fell loosely to their pants pockets, shirttails not quite covering handguns holstered at their sides. Schmidt eyed them carefully, as did Quinton.

Expressions more protective than aggressive, Quinton thought, looking for signs of an assassin's body language. Instead, the men were scanning the perimeter of the *porte-cochere*, peering nonchalantly around the palm trees and the large stucco columns. A light-colored sedan pulled up slowly behind the last Rover, stopped under the overhang, and the men nodded in recognition at the driver and his passenger. Doors opened, and two more men in the sedan, also armed and dressed casually, stepped from the car and onto the brick pavement. The driver removed his sunglasses, and as if on cue, the passenger did the same. Now there were five men actively engaged in lookout duties.

Lake Schmidt helped Mark Adrian out of the SUV, as Steve Farber and Carey Price piled out the other side. From the rear of the sedan,

Fareid gracefully extracted his large frame and buttoned his suit coat. Without a word to the armed men, he joined his friends.

While the group had huddled together waiting for Fareid, Quinton had watched the protective detail as they moved about the driveway area, attracting curious onlookers hoping to learn who might have made such an entrance. Approached by the armed men, the inquisitive quickly lost interest in the bustling arrival and moved on.

"A difficult day, my friends," Fareid said, his right arm resting lightly on Adrian's shoulder. "As you noticed, I'm sure," he said, surveying the armed men, "we will now be moving about the country with a few new associates. There will not be a repeat of this morning's violent event. May I suggest we relax this afternoon, enjoy some quiet time, then meet in the rooftop bar? Steve and Carey, might you help Mark to his room?" Then to Adrian, "Mark, you are recovering very well, my friend. We want to make sure there is no relapse. Shellfish poison is no trifle."

Adrian looked at Fareid and the rest of the group, and said, "I'm feeling better. I'll not continue to be a burden. Know I have been." He adjusted his tortoise shell glasses with both hands, then smoothed his hair back, fingers extended, massaging his scalp. Taking a deep breath, he collected himself and followed his friends toward the elevator in the lobby. Farber and Price walked slowly ahead, letting Adrian set the pace.

The caregivers and their charge entered the lift and disappeared behind the brass doors, which closed in a whoosh. Fareid followed their progress without looking at Quinton and Schmidt. When the elevator was on its way, Fareid turned to the pair, who had also followed the short journey of their colleagues.

"Quinton Schmidt Communications International needs a meeting with its silent partner. The tragic event of today notwithstanding, QSCI has opportunities for great success with the support of the President."

"Shall we convene in your room, as there is a smoking balcony there?" Schmidt asked.

"You are too kind, my professor, but yes that will help me think. I so regret this filthy habit."

The trio moved across the lobby, Fareid patting his pockets in search of the cigarette packet. He pushed the elevator button to take them up. In the elevator, Schmidt asked, "Are we safe to talk in your room? Daniel and I are worried we may have uninvited ears attending our private talks."

"On the balcony, with music on and the shower running, we will have privacy."

"We should be able to . . ." Quinton stopped in mid-sentence as the elevator door opened, and a hotel staff member stood in the opening, leaning on his cleaning cart and gripping a trash bag with his free hand.

Fareid and Quinton stepped around the obstructing cart and strode toward the hotel room down the hall. To the man with the cart, Schmidt said, "*Bon jour* . . . and when he was able to make out the man's nametag, added, "Gonflé."

Fareid halted in mid-stride and grabbed Quinton by the arm.

"Please take my key, Daniel, and wait for me in the suite, room 1245." He turned quickly and with long strides headed for the elevator. Passing a quizzical Schmidt, he said, "I won't be a moment, my professor. Please meet me in my room."

Fareid thrust his hand into the small gap between the elevator doors just before they were to close. They reopened, and Fareid stepped inside.

Gonflé Bevue was preparing to take off his uniform shirt when the door to the elevator opened with a rush. Opposite the elevator, floor-to-ceiling windows filled with sunlight framed a silhouette of a large figure that filled up the doorframe. The door closed, and the figure continued to face the corner of the elevator where Bevue stood. The smaller man was now starting to feel uneasy. *Most people turn around and face the door,* he thought in an instant; then, *Oh God!* as Fareid reached over slowly to the control panel and pressed the large red 'STOP' button. The elevator clanked to a halt between floors. The lights dimmed momentarily, then came back on.

Now the face of Fareid Chamoun was inches away from his own. Bevue felt a giant hand enclose his left wrist in an iron grip, and as he involuntarily gasped, he heard, "Monsieur Bevue, stay perfectly still. Do not move one inch. Not one inch." Bevue quickly nodded in agreement.

"I know who you are, my little friend," Fareid said in a low and deliberate voice. "In fact, I know many things." The grip on Bevue's wrist tightened, and Fareid closed to within a finger's width of the terrified man's face.

"I know your very young girl friend who lives not far from your wife's family." Bevue's eyes now expanded in fear. His heart was about to explode from his chest. "She is still in school, Gonflé. A girl that young with someone . . . like you." Fareid shook his head slowly. "The policemen, powerful men who have the dark cells in a remote detention center, hate this kind of behavior. But maybe not as much as your wife's family will hate it." Fareid took a deep breath and exhaled in Bevue's face, making him blink rapidly.

"What do you want?" Bevue whimpered.

"The names of the men who employ you. And where they live."

"I don't know their names or where they are!" Bevue had no room to escape the face that was inches away. He squirmed slightly, and as he did, Fareid placed his left hand on Bevue's chest and began pushing slowly. A heavy, constantly increasing pressure squeezed the air out of the little man. Bevue's eyes began to bulge even more.

"Shh, my Gonflé." Fareid's admonition whistled around his forefinger, which he had raised to his lips. "You should be quiet just before death."

"Wait!" Bevue gasped, the word barely audible.

Fareid relaxed the pressure, but kept his hand in place. Bevue breathed deeply, unable to speak, his eyes closed.

"Take your time."

"They will . . . kill me . . . if they find out," Bevue said, rasping and clutching the elevator rails.

"They will never have the opportunity to find out, my friend."

"I have only seen one—DuLang, the African man. First name, I don't know. He came as the doctor, the doctor with the pad around his neck." Bevue was starting to breathe better now, but Fareid's hand remained in place. "I told the real doctor who came later he was not needed."

"And?"

"And DuLang's boss is called Ballieux. European. French, maybe Belgian. I don't know. DuLang says he is not only ugly, but a mean and violent man."

"How do you contact them?"

"By telephone, but only through the hotel operator." Bevue then added, hoping to deflect Fareid's focus, "They pay me very little."

Fareid reapplied the pressure, helping Bevue concentrate, and said, "I will pay you better, but here is what you must do: Continue to watch the hotel and report to those two as before. Do nothing, *nothing* different. Soon, I will give you instructions."

"You will pay me better?" Bevue asked.

Fareid said softly, "Yes, I will pay you much better: I am not ugly like this Ballieux, but I am much more violent. So first, my friend, I will not kill you. Second, I will not post the letters that tell your wife's family—she has four older brothers, *n'est ce pas?*—that you have an unhealthy relationship with a schoolgirl."

Fareid drew his left hand away, and Bevue slumped to a crouch, then fell to his knees behind the utility cart. He stared blankly as Fareid pressed the red button to re-energize the elevator, and the machinery hummed into action, taking the lift on its climb back to the twelfth floor. As the door opened, Fareid turned and said, "Remember, do nothing different, and I will be in touch."

Bevue nodded weakly, staring at the back of the cart.

Fareid started out the door, then turned again. "One more thing, Gonflé. Up here. Look at me." Fareid waited for eye contact, then said, "The schoolgirl?" He wagged his forefinger side to side, "Not for you. Not ever." Making sure Bevue got the message, he dragged his thumb across his own throat.

Fareid pushed the button for basement level, moved quietly out the door, and left Bevue to his ignominious ride down.

CHAPTER TWENTY

SCHMIDT HAD LEFT one of the suite's double doors partially opened, and the two men could hear Fareid approaching from the far end of the hallway.

"What was that all about?' Quinton asked, motioning toward the door.

"Not sure, Daniel. Hard to know with Fareid. A lot going on there." Schmidt walked across the room to greet Chamoun.

"Everything OK?" he asked as Fareid came into the room.

"Yes, of course, my professor. My apologies, but I would like a cigarette. May we sit on the balcony?" Fareid made a twisting motion with his hand at Quinton, cocking his head toward the bathroom, then motioned for Schmidt to turn on the television. The shower curtain rustled in the bathroom, and the water began splashing against the tile floor. Schmidt flicked through the channels of the black and white TV, and settled on an African-Cuban combo blaring out a high-energy piece to an enraptured crowd. Fareid nodded, then motioned his friends outside.

When the three men had pulled up chairs and were looking out over the river, Fareid lit up and, each word punctuated by a whiff of smoke, said, "The President has agreed to retain us for one year." Quinton and Schmidt immediately brightened, both leaning forward, eager for the details.

"We have done well in establishing ourselves here with the possibility we may do well beyond imagining." Fareid was relaxed now. He sat back and watched the excitement building in his partners. As he tilted his head back, he took a long pull on his cigarette. He looked out over the tops of the palm trees toward Zaire.

"Sweet Mary, Fareid!" Quinton was on the edge of his chair. "Will you fill in some blanks here?" Schmidt nodded in agreement.

Fareid smiled casually, enjoying the tension. He looked from one partner to the other, then began laughing a deep, frame-shaking laugh. "Yes my friends, we are on the move!"

"Here is what we have—first, a professional wage; for a year we might live as we should." *If Fareid thinks that, then we're in good shape for awhile*, Quinton thought. Schmidt's eyes enlarged.

"But the home run, as you say, is the 'recovery project.'"

Now both Quinton and Schmidt were leaning forward.

"While Denis Sassou-Nguesso was interim President, millions of dollars from oil leases disappeared. Some modest graft is not unusual, but Bissoula and his advisors believe that as much as $800 million went overseas. Our project is to recover as much of that as we can for the government."

"QSCI," Fareid spread his arms to include the entire population of the balcony, "will, of course, charge a fee."

"And you have a formula for that fee," Schmidt suggested.

"I do, my professor, a very simple one. Five million is recovered, our fee is one million; 10 million, our fee is three million; 50 million our fee is ten million, and so forth . . . we recover 800 million, our fee is 100 million. Very simple."

Quinton and Schmidt sat motionless. Each looked at Fareid to see if this were more of his good-natured tormenting. He returned their stare. "Well, my friends?"

After a long silence, Schmidt finally said, quietly, "Did Bissoula agree to this?"

"Of course! This is how business is done!" Fareid said with a flourish, flipping his cigarette butt over the balcony to send it somersaulting to the gardens below.

"Jesus Tapdancin' Christ!" Quinton cried out, "no wonder I live in a one room apartment! I couldn't do the math!"

Schmidt started laughing, joined by first Quinton, then Fareid. Soon, all three had joined in a chorus of hilarity, shouting, "Yes! Of course it's the math! The math!"

When the three men had finally wound down from rerunning the recovery formula for the project (*Projet Monet,* Schmidt had tagged it), they eased into dining in the rooftop café with the rest of the delegation. Leaving the others still working to bring Mark Adrian back to normalcy, the three gathered in Lake Schmidt's room.

"Where do we even begin with this?" Quinton asked Schmidt.

Fareid: "Yes, hmmm."

"Kroll. Jules Kroll." Schmidt said, and waited for the others to ask him what the hell he was talking about. No one bit.

Resigned to addressing this unresponsive classroom of under-graduates, Schmidt licked his forefinger and rose to walk toward the window. In lecture-hall voice, he started, "Jules Kroll, Kroll Associates, Inc., New York City. White-collar crime detective. He assembled legions of accountants, former prosecutors, and law enforcement officers, and focused them on international banking forensics. Kroll's team was able to trace untraceable funds stolen by rogues and blackguards in positions of power. Larceny on a grand scale from all quarters of the globe.

"His most renowned case? The one that made his reputation?" Schmidt tried again. Nothing. "The Ferdinand and Imelda Marcos recovery. And I'm not talking about her shoes.

"No, the recovery of cash stolen during the course of *his* tenure as head of the Philippine government, and *her* reign as the Empress of Acquisition." Schmidt continued, "Bank accounts in New York, Paris, Zurich . . ."

"All the capitals of Europe," Quinton added.

"There, and offshore islands, and on and on."

Fareid: "Was Kroll successful?"

"Evidently so. Although the amount of assets recovered have not been made public, the government of the Philippines was pleased enough that Kroll was able to move into larger offices."

"He's our man, then." Quinton looked to Fareid for agreement.

Fareid nodded at Quinton, "You and Lake should make the first contact. I must stay in the low profile, but will attend as an 'advisor' at the meeting. Do you agree, my professor?"

Schmidt: "I do. Not sure Kroll would send someone to Brazzaville, though. We may have to go to New York."

"In that meeting, with the possibility of an agreement, Bissoula will want to be represented by a very senior government official—the Minister of Oil, or maybe even the Foreign Minister," Fareid said. He stood slowly, then turned and moved toward the far side of the balcony, patting his clothing in search of his pack of Marlboros. He pulled a collapsed red and white box out of his shirt pocket, rattled it a bit, and flipped the lid open to pop out the last cigarette. "Maybe in Zurich or Paris, hmm?" Fareid's gold Cartier lighter wheezed butane, caught the spark and brought flame to a cupped hand. "Yes, Paris." He exhaled. He turned toward Quinton and Schmidt with a look that said *Disagree if all that has transpired is not genius . . .*

Schmidt and Quinton rose and moved to the balcony railing. Quinton said, "We, sir, are not worthy," bowing toward Fareid, arms raised then lowered in the manner of Egyptian slaves. He smiled broadly and added, "And you *are* goddamn brilliant."

"And from my perspective, *pour Projet Monet, Paris est parfait!*" Schmidt grabbed the railing with both hands. "That will be all for today. Class dismissed."

Fareid and Quinton grinned at each other, and the big man turned toward the sliding glass door. He was out of cigarettes.

CHAPTER TWENTY-ONE

MME. BADOUN CAREFULLY moved the file folders and penholders on her desk. She was waiting for the door to the presidential office to open, and when it did in the late afternoon, the rest of the staff gone, she found herself alone with Pascal Bissoula.

"We need to be alone. I have missed you and need your touch," she said, moving closer, removing her suit jacket. Her silk blouse was partially unbuttoned, revealing firm breasts pressing against the expensive fabric. "We are quite alone," she breathed slowly, grabbing Bissoula's hand and placing it inside her shirt on her rib cage.

"Regrettably, my dearest, we must devote the next two hours to ensuring that our Lebanese friend will deliver on his promise to bring the principals of Occidental Petroleum to our cause." The President withdrew his hand from inside Madame's shirt and cupped his palms around her uplifted face. "Later tonight, when the lioness sleeps . . ."

"She never sleeps, Pascal! Your lioness is always awake. We don't have any time now like the old days!" Badoun stepped back and tucked her blouse back into her skirt; the suit jacket came whipping off the back of the chair and swung around her shoulders. She settled in behind her desk, positioning in front of the typewriter. Badoun then snatched a blank piece of paper from a stack beside the machine, twisted it into the Selectric II and asked, "What are your orders, Excellency?"

"Marie," Bissoula said quietly, "there will be time. But now I need you to bring all your resources to bear on ensuring our survival. And please make no mistake; the stakes could not be higher."

Badoun relaxed slightly, almost imperceptibly, and staring straight ahead, said, "Of course you are right, Excellency. Please forgive me."

"*Merci, ma cherie.*" Bissoula turned toward the tall window on the far side of the room, hands clasped behind his back. "PRIVATE AND CONFIDENTIAL" he began, "VIA DIPLOMATIC POUCH to the Embassy of the United States of America, Brazzaville, Congo. EYES ONLY for Ambassador Davidson."

Mme. Badoun sat more erect in her chair and focused on the task at hand, her annoyance at being rebuffed not completely forgotten, but on the way.

"Letter to Dr. Ray R. Irabi, President and CEO, Occidental Petroleum" Bissoula waited, then: "Dear Dr. Irabi, My very kindest regards to you and your family . . ." Mme. Badoun began typing away, stealing a glance at the back of the President as he paced back and forth in front of the window. He paused, inhaled deeply, held and then exhaled slowly through pursed lips. His hands came to his face, then straight back over his forehead and hairline, coming to rest clasped behind his neck.

His hands fell to his side, and he continued, "Your generous offer to enter preliminary discussions concerning oil leases in Congo-Brazzaville, inland and offshore, was intriguing and comes at a crucial time for my government."

"Strike 'generous' and just say 'your offer'," Bissoula corrected.

"While your interest in developing petroleum reserves in my country is acknowledged, my government is in a contractual relationship with ELF Aquitaine relative to most commercially-viable mineral resources. It is a long-standing association, and one I am obliged to honor. Under other circumstances, your overture would be most welcome."

Bissoula paused again. "Should the need arise to reassess current agreements by reason of emergent national economic interests, my Foreign Minister, His Excellency, Monsieur Maurice Goamu, will communicate with your office through the American Embassy here in Brazzaville."

"Finish with all the appropriate courtesies, Marie," Bissoula said, waving his hand. He crossed the room again, then slumped into the wingback chair in the only dark corner of the chamber. "Make sure you put the highest security classification on the document, double seal the file, and hand carry it to our most trusted courier. Have him personally confirm and time-stamp a receipt when delivery is made to the Embassy."

Mme. Badoun nodded while she put the finishing touches on the communiqué.

"Thank you, Marie. This must be kept secret. It is most sensitive and most urgent." Bissoula sat back, leaned his head against the silk-embroidered headrest of the chair, and closed his eyes. *Good,* he thought, *even with all these precautions, ELF will know of this within the hour.*

When the telephone rang, DuLang was in the kitchen wiping the counters with a dishrag. "Always I get to clean up after the pig," he muttered to himself. A half-eaten chicken breast sat molding in the sink, a cigarette butt stubbed out in what little meat remained on the bone. He swatted at one of the many flies on patrol in the cramped cooking space. "*Merde!* I hate this work. If I didn't need the money right away, any other work . . ." DuLang's voice trailed off. He heard Ballieux answer the phone in the living room, kicking an empty wine bottle lying on the floor in the process.

"'Allo," Ballieux grunted into the receiver. "*Oui.*" He paused and listened. Once again, "*Oui.*" Then: "DuLang, you idiot! In here. Now!"

On his way out of the kitchen, Dulang took another swipe at a fly, which through sheer bad timing, succumbed to the dishtowel and landed on the floor, spinning on its back. DuLang, surprised at his prowess, stepped on the insect. As he twisted his foot to grind the little buzzer into mush, he stared at his death-dealing shoe and whispered at it hoarsely, "Ballieux!"

"DuLang!" from the other room.

"Coming!" DuLang called back. "Coming, you sub-human mound of filth," he mumbled, scraping the bottom of his shoe to rid himself of the dead pest.

Ballieux covered the phone and said, "It is that lard-ass Danou, and he is very angry!" He resumed speaking into the receiver: "But of course, Monsieur Danou. We will not fail this time. *Oui.* I understand. *Oui.* Although there must have been some effect from . . ." Ballieux was cut off in mid sentence. DuLang could hear a man's raised voice on the other end of the line. Ballieux remained stoic, choosing to let Danou rail in his ear rather than have DuLang know he was being administered a first class beat-down by his handler.

"Very well," Ballieux said, and hung up the phone.

"Danou? Georges Danou from ELF?" DuLang asked. Now the smaller man wished kitchen cleaning was the extent of his involvement in the enterprise. *This will end badly*, he thought.

"What have we done?"

"It is what we have *not* done, my inept lump of a trainee." Ballieux moved around the couch and picked up a cigarette butt from the ashtray on the coffee table. He made a pass at straightening out the burned end, then lit it from a matchbook he held with one hand. DuLang took a step back from the sulphur and stale tobacco cloud that Ballieux exhaled into the room. "Now, we must finish our job of discouraging the Americans. But, more importantly, retarded one, we must remove that Lebanese meddler from the region, if not this life." Ballieux took a final drag on the cigarette butt, then stamped it out on the linoleum floor.

"He has crossed the line, this pestilence from the Middle East. Chamoun is undermining ELF by bringing in American oil interests. When you undermine ELF, you undermine France and French Africa. Then, the world changes, and we lose our jobs, or worse."

"Worse?"

"Worse, DuLang. How well do you function without kneecaps or testicles?"

Dulang collapsed into the threadbare easy chair that rested on three legs and a pile of magazines, and plopped his head into his hands. "About as well as I am functioning now," he muttered.

"What did you say?"

"Nothing. Nothing at all."

A little more challenging in Brazzaville through the hotel operator, but manageable, Lake Schmidt thought. The effort first to find a telephone number for Kroll Associates in New York, then coordinate the connection with the M'Bamou Palace switchboard, required hours. Timing the call so someone would be in to answer at the Kroll offices took many attempts, and a persistence that was common only in those who found hours of urban statistical research compelling and satisfying.

Schmidt hung up the phone resting on the sideboard in Fareid's suite. He turned to his partners on the sofa, and with a barely stifled air of triumph said, "The train has left the station for Gare du Nord."

Quinton turned briefly toward Fareid, then back to Schmidt. Fareid said: "Professor?"

"What is the next step, you might ask. Well, let me bring you up to the present." Schmidt walked toward the balcony, then turned to face his friends. "We have a meeting in Paris with the head of Kroll's European operation."

"But first . . ." Fareid said.

"Yes," Schmidt acknowledged Fareid's insight with a nod of his head, "first we have to provide Bona Fides for QSCI, including documentary evidence we do, in fact, represent the President of the Congo.

"Fareid, the Master," again a Schmidt head bob, "should be able to procure the same from Mme. Marie Badoun with but a *petite* splash from his vast reservoir of flair."

Fareid accepted the accolade with lowered head and hand on heart, "My professor, you are too kind."

"Yeah, yeah, yeah," Quinton said, "And in the meantime, might we press ahead with the Kroll European guy? Ol' what's-his-beret in Paris?"

"We might, indeed. Fareid, how long with Mme. Badoun?"

"If Kroll will accept a fax with a, what do you say, a 'hard' copy to follow by post, it will be on their desk tomorrow evening."

"I believe that will work. Daniel, I have the number for Hamilton Berger, Kroll's man in Paris. Will you make the call and set up the meeting?"

"I will, as long as you tell me his secretary isn't named Della Rue."

Schmidt shook his head. "From an old TV detective show, Fareid. Not really worth explaining."

CHAPTER
TWENTY-TWO

TWENTY OR SO hotel guests roamed around the pool area in light dappled by overhanging mimosa trees and palm fronds. They prowled about the breakfast buffet table like a pride of lions sensing a herd of wildebeest just a whiff away. The guests made an unconvincing effort to appear relaxed and casual while positioning for the swoop.

The outfits of the patrons tagged their nationalities: Germans with oiled bodies in tight fitting swimsuits, their women in ambitiously skimpy bikinis that failed to restrain the strudel handles hanging over the spandex; men with racing briefs inexplicably small and tight. The Brits with shockingly white skin, exposed unashamedly; the men in plaid shorts with darks socks above suede slip-ons; the ladies in swaths of ephemeral scarves which failed to obscure unfortunate swimsuit selections and the bobbledy legs carrying them staunchly to the breakfast table.

On the far side of the pool under a Cinzano umbrella sat three men wearing variations on a theme of the universal flowered aloha shirt. Two of them had caps, one an Atlanta Braves baseball hat, the other, a sun visor inscribed *Fish On!* The third man sat bareheaded, and wore small clip-on sunshades over a pair of wire rim glasses. They had eaten breakfast earlier and now seemed content to sip and fiddle with espresso cups and observe the passing parade. One of the men pushed a small lemon peel around the table top like a chess piece.

Carey Price picked up the small yellow slice he'd been maneuvering and put it back in the cup saucer. "While the boys are in Paris, I'd like to shoot some photos of the river. Maybe finesse my way onto one of those airboats."

From their table, the Americans could hear the huge turbo fans on the prototype airboat that sat moored to a work dock on the north bank of the river, accelerating and decelerating. Testing had been going on most of the morning.

Farber adjusted his sunglasses, and said, "Not sure they're ready for passengers, Carey. Maybe they see their fleet as matching those glass-covered dinner boats meandering up the Seine, but from what I've seen, the Congo River is not the Seine. Maybe a good photo would be the crew working on those monster fans."

Mark Adrian agreed. "Maybe the best perspective for shots of the river is from the top of the hotel. Me, I'm fascinated by the gardens on the grounds. I've seen a collection of English-language booklets in the lobby about the variety of plants that are here. Right here in the gardens of the hotel."

"Hope the books have pictures." Price goaded Adrian, looking for some sign the man with the Atlanta Braves hat would push back, giving his friends a sense that he was on his way to a full recovery.

"Me too," replied Adrian, "'cause I can't read. But I might press Dr. Nguomo into service. Maybe he'll take pity and read for the literacy-challenged tourist. He's paying a follow-up visit this afternoon."

Price and Farber exchanged looks. "One or both of us ought to be there when he comes, don't you think, Mark?" Price offered.

"Fine idea," Farber concurred. "Although Fareid didn't say anything, I had the sense he had strong reservations about our Dr. Nguomo. Wish to hell we'd asked Fareid about another visit from this guy. Daniel's initial inquiries with World Health didn't reveal anything. At the first pass, they couldn't find a record of our Dr. Nguomo.

"Well, it is an international organization operating in Africa," Price said. "Can't imagine World Health has much better record keeping than a stateside DMV, and you know how that works."

"True, his name could be wallowed in the mire. I'll get his business card during the next visit," Adrian said. "He seemed harmless enough, although no Albert Schweitzer." Adrian turned his chair to face the gardens between the pool and the terrain that down sloped to the river. "I'll be fine. Steve aren't you working on an interview with the President?"

"I am, Mark. Mme. Badoun appears to be the gatekeeper on my request, and her gate opens very slowly. I need Fareid's oily good manners and charm; simply don't have it. I'll have to rely on the care of French-trained bureaucrats."

"Might want to pick an alternate subject for your piece, in that case," Price remarked.

"Well, gentlemen," Mark said, "I'm off to the hotel library to gather up some literature on those provocative twin sisters, flora and fauna. Dr. Nguomo at 3:00; then drinks in the roof top bar?"

"Perfection. And stay away from shrimp plants, Mark," Steve added, but Adrian had already turned and headed for the lobby.

After Mark Adrian had left the other men outside and found himself thumbing through the leaflets stuck in a mahogany display case, it occurred to him that his appointment with the World Health doctor had not been confirmed for place. Time was 3:00 p.m. certain enough, but where they would meet was still unclear.

Just then, Adrian could see, across and outside the lobby, someone looking much like Nguomo speaking with a shorter man. The Nguomo figure was of a height and build of the doctor, wore African tribal dress, but no neck brace or glasses. The man with whom he spoke Adrian had seen many times near the front doors of the hotel, recognizable by the dragon shirts he preferred.

The two were conversing heatedly, the shorter man wagging his finger, lecturing without pause. The Nguomo figure stood still and mute, waiting for Dragon Shirt to quit breathing fire. Apparently with no satisfaction from the recipient, the fire breather turned on his heel and departed, leaving the other man stranded in his solitude.

Shoulders slumping after the verbal caning, the man checked his watch, then reached in the bag that lay in a heap next to him and pulled out a neck brace. From his coat pocket he pulled some thick black-frame glasses. Dr. Fulbert DuLang Nguomo gathered himself to his full height, and walked toward the lobby, careful to peer under his lenses to avoid tripping on anything in his path.

During the animated exchange between the two men, Adrian had dropped into the seat on the round sofa where Dr. Nguomo had first treated him. He raised his hand as the now fully-accessorized doctor made his way into the lobby. Dr. Nguomo spotted him immediately and waved in recognition.

"Well, well, Mr. Adrian," Nguomo said. He took a seat next to the American, and added, "You are looking much improved!"

"As you are, Doctor," Adrian said stiffly. "Appears neither your neck brace nor your glasses are needed that much. Your ailments must be far less troubling than when we met the other night."

Nguomo sat stone still. His eyes moved left, then right, to take in all who were nearby in the lobby, particularly those who showed even a passing interest in their meeting.

"Some days are better than others," DuLang said unconvincingly. "But you—have you any residual symptoms?"

"My friend, whoever you are, you can't possibly imagine I still think you're a doctor, can you?" Adrian stared at the dazed man and lightly touched the temple of his glasses. Working at maintaining his composure, he continued, "You can dispense with those ridiculous props. No thanks to you, I am actually feeling better, but I sense that was not the outcome you intended. Am I right?" Adrian could feel his bile rising in spite of his best efforts to control it. Red blotches that had receded into memory were in danger of returning.

DuLang shook his head vigorously, squeezing his eyebrows in disagreement, but then dropped his head into his hands and massaged his face, the thick glasses ending up on the top of his head. "How has this happened?" The Velcro binder that held the neck brace made a slow ripping sound as he removed it. Dulang dejectedly dropped it to the floor.

He raised his face and looked at Adrian, and said, "I didn't think that 'just making you sick' was really hurting you. I was supposed to make you want to leave, you and the other Americans, by using the castor beans."

Dulang returned to rubbing his face. "But my God, how did I become that man who would think such a thing?

"And my name is Fulbert DuLang."

"DuLang? Castor beans?" Adrian looked at DuLang, then across the gardens he could see through the lobby window. "They're here in the hotel garden, but I had no idea they were . . ."

"Poisonous? Yes, when reduced, they become the deadly poison ricin. And that was what I was to inject into you the other night." DuLang hung his head, then looked out into the garden. "I am sorry I agreed to do that to you."

Adrian said, "Agreed? With whom did you agree to inject ricin into a complete stranger, a guest in your country? Someone who has done no harm and wants to create jobs for your countrymen! For God's sake man!"

Dulang rose and took a step back from Adrian, who sat stunned and angry. Neither man could face one another. DuLang finally took a step forward and said, "That is what you Americans want, but everybody doesn't always want what you want, even though it may seem like a good thing."

"But to murder someone if you disagree? And what about that innocent woman in the market place?"

"That was an accident. Ballieux, he . . ." Dulang stopped himself, then continued, "He was too aggressive, and that was not supposed to happen. It was unforgivable.

"But, I can tell you, Mark Adrian, if you go to the authorities and tell them what we've talked about, it will not end well. There are elements in Bissoula's government who do not want you here. They will let powerful people soil their hands while they stay in the background claiming it is a commercial dispute that has turned criminal. Of course headlines will be *All Efforts Made to Apprehend the Evildoers, These Gunmen Destroy Economic Opportunity,* and so on.*"*

Dulang was pacing now, alternately wringing his hands, then throwing them in the air in surrender. "You know how that will go. There is very little you can do at this point, Mark Adrian, but to buy some African street art, enjoy the fresh fruit, and then go home and tell your friends tales of the Congo. That is the best possible outcome!"

"I am not an appreciator of African art, or any art for that matter, and I'm about up to my hat brim in fresh fruit. I'm afraid to eat anything, especially if it swims."

Adrian stood and blocked DuLang from pacing. "We will be leaving eventually, all of us, Fulbert, but I think I speak for the delegation when I say we will not leave under duress."

DuLang carried on: "And Fareid? What are his intentions with Occidental Petroleum? They will not be welcomed by ELF Aquitaine, I assure you."

"I know nothing of this." Adrian sat up straight, and said, "ELF Aquitaine? Is that who you are involved with? You started to mention a Balli or Ballieu. Is he the ELF agent who wanted you to murder me?"

"Not murder. Influence. It was almost a joke! We laughed about it."

"A joke? Yeah, you were laughing and I was blowing up like a red snapper hooked to a bicycle pump!"

"That was the shrimp, not me." DuLang looked away from Adrian, then added quietly, "But I did try to make it worse."

"With ricin? I guess so. A lot worse!" Adrian took off his glasses and cleaned them with his front shirttail. "Fulbert, let me ask you. How are you going to get away from this pig you are involved with?"

"I don't know. I don't know." DuLang stared over Adrian's shoulder. The far side of the lobby was open toward the pool, and he could see just a slice of the river, and beyond.

"I have a friend in Zaire. But no work. Ballieux . . . ." DuLang realized he had given up the name again, and noticed Adrian's reaction. "Yes, Ballieux, Laurent Ballieux. That is the pig. He will find me and kill me."

Adrian stared at the distraught man, and could offer neither advice nor solace. "I don't know what to tell you. But what I will do when Fareid returns from Paris is make sure he knows you have tried to help us. Maybe he will have an idea."

DuLang shook his head slowly. "No, there is no idea that is good. You must leave; you must go. Even if oil is not involved, ELF does not welcome an American presence. It doesn't matter what the official government position is.

"I hope you return safely to Atlanta, Mark Adrian. I hope your team wins the Cup," Dulang said pointing with his chin at Adrian's baseball cap. "But mostly I hope you return safely to your country." He gathered up his swirl of brightly patterned fabric, re-centered his braided cap, then turned and walked toward the front doors. His sandals slapped quietly on the marble floor as he made his way to the exit.

"Wait a second," Adrian called out, and followed after him.

On the far side of the pool terrace under a mango tree heavy with fruit, a man wearing military sunglasses sipped from a tall glass. He had watched the meeting in the lobby between Adrian and DuLang, and although it was at least 75 yards away, he was confident he knew what was being said. He dropped his cigarette in what remained of the orange-yellow punch and waved impatiently to the waiter. As the young man in the white and gold jacket hustled over to the table, the man arose from his chair, dropped a bank note on the table next to his glass, and brushed past the startled waiter holding his bar tab. "And thank you, Monsieur Ballieux. Enjoy the day," he murmured, glaring at the back of the retreating hulk of surliness.

CHAPTER
TWENTY-THREE

PROCESSING THROUGH CUSTOMS at Charles de Gaulle had been painless; the three men arriving from the Congo had but one suitcase apiece, and their documents had been in order. They piled into one of the waiting taxis and pulled out onto the Autoroute du Nord, with Fareid and the driver exchanging comments in French about how terrible the traffic was.

Fareid turned to Quinton and Schmidt, and said, "You will enjoy my cousin's hotel, The Royal Monceau. It is just south of Parc Monceau on Avenue Hoche." He turned to the driver, "'Walking distance to L'Arc de Triomphe, is it not?"

"*Oui, Monsieur,* it is a beautiful hotel! The bathroom floors are marble, but the hot water, how do you say, *peeps?* run through the floor so Madame's feet do not get the chill!"

"Perfect," Quinton said. "No one gets cold feet." He looked at Fareid in the front seat, then, for the second time, saw a green Peugeot in the side view mirror. "Do we have many turns to make before the hotel, Fareid, because I think we've been tagged? We're being followed."

Schmidt peered out the driver's window to see if he could make out the car in the left mirror, as Fareid looked casually out the front side window, and then back quickly to the driver. The taxi had just eased into the traffic on Avenue de Chapelle, when Fareid said calmly to the cabbie, "Pull over, if you would, at the first tobacco shop. There." He pointed to a tobacconist's on the corner. "And pull around the side, please."

The car came to a stop after making the turn, and Fareid felt for his wallet while he watched the green Peugeot roll past them. Fareid continued his self-pat down as he eyed the tailing car and its right front seat passenger, following their progress until the sedan pulled over three car spaces ahead.

"Fareid . . ." Quinton began, but before he could finish, Fareid said, "The passenger, Daniel? Professor? Imagine him in a khaki bush jacket."

Schmidt exclaimed, "Yes! The sunglasses and unshaven face."

Quinton: "That's him, the ugly piece of garbage!"

"Please, stay here."

Fareid pulled himself out of the taxi and headed down the street, looking in shops as he went. When he came abreast of the Peugeot, he turned sharply and knelt by the front passenger door, blocking the occupant from opening it, staring at him face on.

The window came down slowly, and the large unkempt head of Laurent Ballieux stared up at Fareid. "Chamoun? May I join you on the sidewalk? We can perhaps have a coffee while your American friends learn more of Paris from the taxi driver."

"Of course, my friend. Allow me . . ."

Fareid opened the door, and as Ballieux's hand grabbed the doorframe to help himself out, Fareid slammed his full weight against the car door, jamming the fat hand and its sausage fingers in a metal press. Ballieux screamed, but before he could make a move, Fareid grabbed the man's yellow tie, made a single wrap with his right hand, and jammed his fist up against the Belgian's throat. Ballieux was pinned in the doorframe with Fareid's sledgehammer of a fist crushing his larynx. His eyes were bulging from the pain of his hand clamped in the door, and panic filled his face, unsure he would ever again draw a clean breath.

"Look at me, you disgusting piece of filth. If I ever see you within sight of me or my friends, or I hear you have been seen in places where we have just visited, or are about to visit, or are just thinking about visiting, I will be very angry." Fareid tightened his necktie stranglehold. Ballieux was turning crimson, rasping for breath. "And I will come after your superior, Danou is it? And he will be very upset. You tell him that, will you please?

"I need to see you nod 'yes,' Ballieux," Fareid said. The up and down head movement was barely perceptible, but Fareid, satisfied, let go of Ballieux's necktie. "You need to now have your driver take you to the infirmary to set those broken fingers." Fareid put his forefinger to his lips to motion silence, then jerked his right thumb, motioning the driver to move off down the street.

The driver of the Peugeot ground the gears and pulled out in front of an oncoming Renault, whose driver sat on the horn and could be heard cursing loudly at the retreating car.

"Hope that was the right guy," Quinton said when Fareid returned to the taxi. Schmidt and his partner had remained in the taxi and witnessed the confrontation in silence, gasping when Fareid had slammed the door on unsuspecting fingers, but otherwise silent, fascinated by the big man's graceful and agile aggression.

'That was the right guy, my friends. He is a Belgian thug, and will be back to haunt us." Fareid settled into the front seat of the taxi and took a cigarette pack from his suit coat pocket. He offered one to the driver, who graciously declined, then turned to the pair in the back seat and said, smiling, "But we will recognize him from his bandaged hand should he decide to throw another banana skin in our path." Fareid turned and faced forward, exhaling a slow stream of smoke through the opening in the passenger window. "This man will be trouble," Fareid said, mostly to himself.

The lobby of the Royal Monceau was modest, but welcoming. It was richly paneled in Honduran mahogany, trimmed with African spice woods and bronze fixtures that, but for the occasional Napoleonic emblem, would lead arriving guests to believe they were entering a private club in Picadilly.

What set the unassuming entrance apart was the staircase that opened up on the far wall. A flight of steps descended, then widened into an elegant atrium a floor below. Comfortable chairs and sofas, some upholstered, some leather, had been placed casually but purposefully in and among palm trees, orchid plants, and bronze floor lamps. These seating areas were designed for small groups of guests, and by their arrangement and protective flora served conspirators well.

Glass and white steel formed a circular skylight high overhead, and the light from the late afternoon sun above Paris bore through the patterned circle above to fill the eastern section of the atrium below with a broad column of light. The sun, having already traversed across the conspiracy islands of the atrium's western section, eased into gray and silver lights that were quickly becoming evening.

In this shaded sector of the room sat Fareid, Quinton and Schmidt. A fourth man sat with them, and listened as Fareid explained the details of *Projet Monet*. His legs were crossed and he sat back in his seat, elbows resting on the arms of his chair. The tailored linen suit he wore looked expensive and was remarkably unrumpled. The way it draped over the man's frame said that its tall, elegant wearer travelled in moneyed circles. His fingers formed a small chapel in front of his nose, through which he peered at the three men.

"Al-Hami, my friend from Cairo. I trust a partner in the law firm of Baker and MacKenzie will be able to find billable hours in the City of Lights." Fareid said, "And running into his old classmate Chamoun is just a pleasant coincidence."

"Pleasant? Yes. Coincidence? No, of course not. You invited me, Fareid. Profitable? We shall place our faith in Allah. Success if He wills it.

"And yes there will be billable hours, but not invoiced to my dear friend and Olympic adversary."

Al-Hami Makel turned to the two Americans and said, "Are you comfortable with the formula your not-so-silent partner has concocted for the recovery of the embezzled funds?"

Quinton answered Makel by querying Schmidt. "Seems fairly reasonable to us, does it not, professor?"

Schmidt: "Less than 5%, Al-Hami, but $30 million to QSCI and its associates accrues only if we, or should I say Kroll, recovers the full $800 million."

Makel addressed the group. "Even for a lawyer, that would be a handsome payday. But to put hundreds of millions back into the coffers of the Congolese government would certainly earn you the lasting gratitude of the President in office at the time. If you are able to proceed apace and start returning the monies to Brazzaville within the year, that

President has a good chance of still being Pascal Bissoula. The man our friend Fareid Chamoun I believe refers to as 'Papa.' And I suspect he would find ways to underwrite further commercial enterprises of your organization."

"You were an Olympian?" Quinton asked Fareid.

Fareid looked at Makel, and said, "Yes, we were on the equestrian teams. Unworthy of coverage by Wide World of Sports, but we did compete and stayed in the Olympic Village. Al-Hami was a superior rider, but I fared better in the cafeteria line. I met his future wife there, who, in spite of my best efforts, took only two days to upgrade from the Lebanese to the Egyptian."

"It was not exactly like that, but I have been very fortunate," Makel countered. "Fareid has led an exciting life and was the much better catch. But he was unable to commit to anything but exotic travel and deal making, so perhaps in this one event, I was the better horseman."

"Back to the formula, Al-Hami," Schmidt said. "Is that enough information to draft an agreement for us to present to the Foreign Minister? One that would have a fair chance of success?"

"Yes, of course."

Fareid: "Good! Tomorrow we meet with His Excellency, Maurice Gaomu and Monsieur Berger from Kroll. The meeting will be at the Hotel Georges V, 8 p.m."

"I see they're travelling as if they had already recovered the $800 million," Quinton said.

"Not really, my friend," Fareid said. "They travel that way always, and even more so when they visit Paris. I promise you, the Foreign Minister's entourage will be numbered in the scores, their shopping efforts will be prodigious, and the booty returning to Brazzaville would fill a Spanish galleon."

Makel scribbled a few more lines in a leather notebook, closed it with precision, and slid the platinum Mont Blanc back into his jacket pocket. He then gathered up his briefcase and light overcoat, and stretched his bony but impeccably-manicured hand out to the two Americans. "A pleasure, Lake and Daniel. Here is to success and prosperity, although that may be a touch redundant."

"Here's to 'em!" Daniel replied.

CHAPTER
TWENTY-FOUR

THE PENSIONE TWO blocks off Avenue Hoche occupied the second and third floors of an inelegant four-story building which couldn't hide its plainness, even with a pale yellow plaster façade. The blue porcelain street sign near the corner of the building was chipped and faded, and the lettering *Rue du Chat qui Peche* was legible only from a few feet away.

The shutters that framed the windows fronting the street were all accounted for, but many of the slats hung at distracting angles and were an unwelcoming omen to all except lodgers seeking the least expensive and most anonymous of quarters.

Ballieux found himself struggling up the stairs against the flow of young students who descended with their olive drab backpacks, smelling of patchouli and spreading agitated pheromones like crop dusters. The young inhabitants greeted him with the collegiality of the proletariat, but he was clearly not a Bohemian, nor a student, nor an artist. He wore his thuggery like a badge, and his foul aura did not invite easy conversation. After their first encounters with the menacing presence, the students avoided any eye contact and found themselves pressing against the opposite wall when he passed.

The lone window in the room rattled in its frame as Ballieux opened the door, dropping his duffel bag on one of the two metal-framed beds that butted up lengthwise against each windowless wall. A doorway led into a small tiled bathroom, and from his position between the beds, the occupant could see a claw-footed bathtub nestled near the toilet. The faucets for the tub were in a standard pensione configuration: the cold water knob in its place; the hot water knob missing. A small placard above the bath informed the bather that, for the convenience of the guest, the knob to the hot water could be leased, for the duration of the bath, from the front desk for five francs. And in consideration to other residents, the knob should be returned as soon as modesty might allow.

Ballieux had unbuttoned his shirt, and was looking at the dark stubble of his unshaven face in the stained mirror. He rubbed his chin with the fingers protruding from his self-bandaged hand. He thought briefly of a coldwater scrape-off, but chose instead to drop his trousers and sit on the toilet.

"Ballieux is once again living like a rat-killer, sorting through garbage," he said to himself. He counted the tiles on the floor as he awaited a good result. How and when he would dispose of Fareid Chamoun presented a problem, but the answer came to him as he stood and buckled his belt. Ballieux was satisfied with the plan and his new lightness of being. "It will be very painful for that big bowl of tabouli. The last face on earth I want him to see is mine, laughing as he meets a miserable end."

The hair salon on the corner of Avenue Hoche and Rue Beaujon was named *Bleu*. It always struck Al-Hami Makel as a bit of Scottish humor in the middle of Paris: The owner and master stylist was a redhead from Campbeltown who had the frame of a rugby player and the hands of an intervention cardiologist. His mates from early days in Scotland had good-naturedly saddled the young man with the shock of hair as red as a fire at night with the nickname "Blue."

The name transferred with the Scotsman when the Paris shop opened, and, as well-heeled Parisiennes increasingly touted it, Makel had made it a mandatory stop while in the city on business. Appointment day at *Bleu* always included a light trim (Makel never let his silvering locks go more than three days without professional attention), scalp massage, manicure, and arguing the merits of saxophonist Stanley Turrentine over Blue's favorite, Charlie Parker.

"Parker was innovative, Blue, but Turrentine played with such finesse!" Blue harrumphed as Makel settled into the restored American Koken barber chair, allowing his feet to rise and his head to recline as the striped barber towel was draped over his silk shirt. Blue, as he did for all long time customers, waved and snapped the lightweight silk with the flair of a matador executing the perfect Veronica. He turned and reached for the lanolin to soften up Makel's beard for the straight razor shave. The salve applied to the elegant chin, Blue picked up his bone-handled Swiss razor, and began the stropping process, slapping back and forth with rhythmic determination.

The only other occupant of the shop was a Sardinian named Vivaldo, who had just swept the shop floor and was taking a smoke break in the alley behind the salon. Makel and Blue were alone when the little coiled bell at the top of the street-side door announced the arrival of another patron. Ballieux had opened the door slowly, his eyes never leaving the man in the chair and the figure hovering around him.

"A few minutes, Monsieur; I just started on this gaffer's treatment, but my associate will be right along to fill your needs. Kindly have a stump, yeah, and we'll be with you shortly. Coffee on the table there." Blue pointed with his chin toward the small marble-top table in front of the chairs in the waiting area, while he administered the last flourishing strokes on the leather strop.

Makel was breathing through a hot, moist towel, waiting for the soothing application of the pre-shave balm and sorting out flight logistics for his return to Cairo the next day. The relaxation was an indulgent but well-earned reward, he thought, for this effort to help his friend Fareid. The likelihood it would also result in a handsome payday was really irrelevant. Makel reasoned: *There are costs associated with my plans to visit an old friend in Pigalle this evening, and I am, after all, a proponent of performance-based compensation. Helping a friend allows me perhaps to help another friend.*

To Makel, all of his activity in Paris this week seemed to have a certain symmetry, a congruency of purpose. To emerge into the evening life of his favorite city impeccably groomed, scented like a boulevardier, and confident of a prosperous result from his noble endeavors was the perfect way to conclude his business.

Makel was contemplating how precisely the universe appeared to be aligned to his preferences when the shiv Ballieux had been hiding in his coat pocket exploded downward through the salon drape into Makel's left rib cage, into his heart cavity, instantly and mortally wounding the Egyptian lawyer. The hot towel jerked upward and sideways as Makel reacted violently to the knife thrust. Ballieux grabbed the wide-eyed man in the throes of his horrible death and pulled his face close, saying, "You should have stayed in Cairo and charmed cobras, my Egyptian lawyer friend. An angry ELF says: Yanqui Go Home."

Ballieux spat, then pounced on the astonished Blue, who had reeled back during the initial attack and was backed up against the porcelain counter. Stunned by the violence of the moment, Blue was defenseless, and in spite of his size, Ballieux was able to grab the straight razor from Blue's grasp and take a vicious swipe at the big Scot's throat. Blue reflexively warded off the blow with his left arm, and the razor was prevented from striking home by the intervention of his tricep, his forearm covering his face. The fleshy underside of Blue's arm took the full rage of a Samurai-style slash meant to deal a deathblow to the throat of the big man, and now that underarm was splayed open like a haggus on Robbie Burn's night. Blue started to scream out, but Ballieux had anticipated the reaction, and shot his hand up to cover the wounded man's mouth.

Outside the salon, the motion of the scuffle in his peripheral vision startled a young passerby. Uncertain of what he was seeing, he leaned toward the salon's front glass, and brought his hands up to the sides of his face as he peered in at the flailing chaos.

In spite of Ballieux's being acutely fixed on killing the big Scot, the change in light coming through the front of the store was enough to distract the attacker for the flash of a second. His head turned slightly, Ballieux could sense the figure in the window, but couldn't see who was witnessing the murder. He knew he now had just seconds to finish his job. Feeling Blue struggle beneath him, he returned to the attack and made a quick lunge with the razor on the exposed side of Blue's head. The sharpened steel caught the back side of the downed man's ear and sliced across the back of his neck, up into his hairline, leaving a deep gash which quickly turned into a rush of blood as thick and dark as a dog's.

The young man on the sidewalk screamed in revulsion and started running eastward toward the intersection of Hoche and Rue Beaujon. Ballieux could hear the man's terrorized screeching and knew he was running not just away from the salon, but toward someone who would respond to the report of horror just witnessed. Blue lay immobile on the granite floor, blood from the slash wounds beginning to pool around his body. Ballieux quickly wiped and folded his razor, and slid it back into his jacket pocket. He took a hurried survey of the kill scene, stepped over Blue's prostrate form, and bent down to wipe clean the ornate ivory handle of the knife that protruded from Al-Hami Makel's lifeless form. "This souvenir I leave for you, Fareid Chamoun."

As the assassin turned toward the door, his foot slipped on the blood that now surrounded the barber chair. There were splatters on the cabinetry under the mirrors, and an ejaculation of blood dots sprayed across the mirror. Ballieux genuflected involuntarily as he recovered his balance. As his right knee touched the bloody floor, he braced himself with his injured hand and the bandage wrapped around his fingers rolled back. The cuts from the car door jam opened afresh, leaving a bloody smudge on the black and white patterned tile. Cursing, he rose and made his way toward the front door. The coiled brass bell on the doorframe sounded as he left.

CHAPTER
TWENTY-FIVE

B Y THE TIME the police arrived at the salon, a small crowd had gathered outside on the sidewalk. Inspector Morain had pressed in behind his Sergeant, who bulled his way through the gawkers to the blood-splattered crime scene. They entered together, the Sergeant covering his mouth and nose with a handkerchief. Emergency Technicians from Hospital Marmottan had raced down Avenue Carnot, around Place Charles de Gaulle, and found themselves at the Avenue Hoche crime scene minutes ahead of the investigators.

Inspector Morain was well known among the beat gendarmes and the EMTs. He was invariably called in on homicide cases of high interest to the public, and was known to the first responders as a quiet but relentless seeker of truth, uncompromising in his search for justice for the victims of violent crimes.

His superiors did not view Morain's methods entirely with approval. The Headquarters Group had been embarrassed by the city press for their public censure of the popular police figure. The Napoleonic Code and rules of evidence must hold sway, they had argued in response. This served to solidify the Inspector's standing among the rank and file, but it did not help Morain's effort to maintain a career-prolonging low profile.

As an accomplished investigator with a long list of successes in complex cases, Morain had been mentioned on and off as a candidate for Commissaire, but his aggressive tactics in the field were overshadowed by his swirling typhoon of a personal life. His stormy relationships outside of the office had left him a runner-up in the competition for the high position more than once. Headquarters Group demanded a balance, insisting that discretely tending to personal matters was an essential component of a detective's professional life. Recurring destructive visits from Morain's third wife to the investigator's office had not improved Morain's chances of advancement. Broken furniture and accessories belonging to the Group had to be paid for and the resulting paperwork was an unwelcome burden.

He rode out his few off-duty days by working hard to contain the firefight between him and his estranged family. Time on duty, by comparison, was quiet and contemplative.

"So it goes," he would suggest to his Sergeant when another eruption of familial sores reddened Morain's complexion.

"That is not the way HQ Group sees it, I'm afraid," his Sergeant would always reply.

As the Inspector slowly moved about the crime scene, the Sergeant and the uniformed police waited for Morain's instructions, which now came in quick bursts: "Sergeant," pointing to his second-in-command, "take three men and gather blood evidence. I want four different samples from each splattering." He pointed: "There on the cabinet, there on the mirror, on the chairs, sheets. Here on the floor. Separate bags and tags.

"I want to know if anyone else may have been involved in this swordplay. Are there other victims perhaps? Maybe the attacker was wounded. Be very precise and cautious with your collection and recording. Everyone in gloves. Now!"

Morain scanned the room, and addressed the remaining uniformed officer: "Check the back room and exit for blood. I want to know if any bleeders left that way. Then dust all the chairs and walls for prints."

He selected a chair from against the back wall of the salon, dusted it carefully, sat and crossed his legs. Pointing now to Vivaldo, who stood in the corner, stupefied by the events that occurred while he was but yards away, Morain said, "Over here, my friend. Come sit." He patted a chair next to him that had been screened, examined, and was now available for use.

"Now, tell me every thing you heard, saw, felt, smelled, and tasted while you were in the back, outside the salon. Every detail. Nothing you remember will be insignificant."

Vivaldo stumbled through the events as best his shaken recollection would allow. He remembered hearing the bell, he said, the tinkling sound advising all in earshot that someone had just arrived. "I wanted to finish my break. I had just lit my cigarette! I thought, *they can wait*, and I stayed outside." While he spoke, he looked away from the front of the salon, first at Morain, then at the back door so he wouldn't have to look at the slaughterhouse in the salon. "I didn't want to be called back to work before my break ended, so I wandered off down the alley."

"All right, Vivaldo, anything else?"

"No! There is nothing, nothing! I could not have helped Señor Blue, and the other man. You see my size? You see how big is Señor

Blue? What could have Vivaldo done? Vivaldo could not have helped!" Vivaldo began rocking back and forth in his chair, his eyes darting back and forth, but still avoiding a look at the gruesome scene beyond the Inspector.

"*D'accord, mon ami.*" Morain rose and stood between the dazed Sardinian and the murder scene. "I regret you will most likely be required to find other work," the Inspector said, further deflating the bewildered man who, still seated, was now holding his knees. "But I can tell you your helping us find this brutal killer will be an excellent recommendation to a future employer. You may use me as a reference," Morain said. He handed Vivaldo his business card.

And I can keep track of you, my timid friend, Morain thought.

A small crowd of watchers had remained outside the salon. Some moved about self-consciously to get a better view of the carnage. There was not much conversation among them, only the occasional quick inhale, or an 'oh!' The crime scene investigators were aware of the observers, but largely ignored them.

Morain moved into the front of the salon from his interview with Vivaldo and noticed the spectators on the sidewalk outside. The Sergeant saw the Inspector looking at the front window, and asked, "Cover the window? There are sheets in the cabinet."

Morain said, "No. I want you to get the photographer and bring him to the front of the salon. Tell him this: Take more photos of the corpses." Morain had turned from the window, and continued, "What I really want are photos of the people on the other side of that glass. The photographer should start shooting with all the subtlety he can muster.

Group shots first, that we can enlarge for detail. Tell him to get as many full facials as possible.

"Then tell two of the uniforms to get names and addresses of everyone on the sidewalk looking in. Ask for ID. Detain them if necessary, and run down any who scatter. I will interview the bolters personally."

The Sergeant moved off without a word to collect those designated by the Inspector. Morain followed, and stopped at the chairs where the personal belongings of the deceased were displayed in orderly groups.

"These belong to this gentleman," the young woman pointed with her gloved hand at the victim with the knife in his chest. On the chair, neatly arranged, were a platinum Mont Blanc fountain pen, a Patek Phillipe wrist watch, an Italian leather wallet, and a fold of francs, US dollars, and Egyptian pounds clasped in a hinged gold and silver money clip. The wallet's contents were fanned out in the woman's hand and held forward for Morain to examine.

"He appears to be an Egyptian; Cairo address." She handed Morain a driver's license and some business cards. "An attorney, it looks like, with the firm Baker, McKenzie."

"Al-Hami Makel," Morain read off the license. He examined the first business card: "Yes, Baker, McKenzie. Over 800 partners. Based in America, I believe, but they are everywhere, like the cockroach." He turned the card over. Nothing on the back.

Flicking through the other items, he stopped at a cream-colored, engraved card that read only

Fareid Chamoun
London, England.

On the reverse of the card, Morain could make out the words in blue-black ink, *Royal Monceau Hotel*, a telephone number, and what appeared to be a room number. He handed all of the cards back to the investigator, save the one with the writing. "Thank you, *mademoiselle*." Morain slipped the card of interest into his jacket breast pocket and continued toward the back of the salon.

CHAPTER TWENTY-SIX

FAREID CHAMOUN, DANIEL Quinton, and Lake Schmidt had been to the Hotel Georges V before, but the lobby always had the same effect on each of them. It wasn't the ornate and gilded statuary and light fixtures, or the haughty air of the front desk staff, or even the priceless 17th century Savonnerie carpet resting with self-importance over polished inlaid marble flooring. It was the seductive air of conspiracy, romance and intrigue that permeated the walls, the furniture, the filtered light from its front bay window.

When Joel Hillman, at a then unprecedented amount of $31 million, built the hotel in 1928, it became an immediate focal point for the *glitterati* of the era. Scott and Zelda Fitzgerald, Cocteau, Hemingway, royals from the House of Windsor, Russian Counts, and aspiring senior government ministers plotted and schemed, dined and imbibed, elbow to elbow in the finest luxury of the day. Their long-ago presence still hung in the atmosphere like gauze—palpable, filmy—disturbing, because it put a new visitor on edge. The space was more than just the sum of the accessories in a cube.

A young Congolese in a loosely-fitting blue suit rose when he spotted the group. He crossed the lobby and approached Fareid with his hand extended. "Monsieur Chamoun, I am Ndono. Michael Ndono from the Foreign Minister's staff. Dr. Schmidt? Cdr. Quinton?" He shook both of the men's hands, and motioned them to a quiet corner of the lobby. "Please, if you will, so we might speak in private.

"The Foreign Minister would be honored if you would be so kind as to meet him and his staff in the fourth floor conference room this evening at 8 p.m. Please bring the Director from Kroll Associates, Mr. James."

Fareid bowed slightly and said, "Monsieur Ndono, we will be equally honored to oblige the Foreign Minister, and look forward to advancing the cause of the Congolese government. We will see you at 8 o'clock as requested. I have advised Robert James we will be meeting this evening. He, too, looks forward to visiting with the Foreign Minister." Fareid bowed slightly, and said, "Till this evening."

As Michael Ndono crossed the lobby, Quinton and Schmidt watched him retreat, then circled around Fareid. "You know what James will demand of the Foreign Minister, don't you Fareid?" Schmidt asked.

"Yes, I do. They're in a strong position, Kroll is, and they will insist on a retainer as a start, in the vicinity of $100,000.00. Sassou-Nguesso absconded with $800 million in oil revenues, and that left very little to run a fledgling government. Bissoula is much in need of a bridge loan for operational funds until he can tap into the stream from ELF Aquitaine." Fareid tapped out a cigarette, then asked of the others: "Will you join me in the garden?"

Quinton and Schmidt rose and accompanied the big man outside onto the back terrace.

When they were seated in chairs under a sprawling laurel tree, Schmidt said, "Unless Kroll can recover significant funds from Paris, Brussels, Monaco, and wherever else Sassou-Nguesso has hidden them, and do so in a hurry, the Bissoula government will be in a considerable bind. And if the project is unsuccessful, some other stop-gap measure will be necessary."

"Not likely in less than a year." Quinton said. "Moreover, ELF agents will be actively discouraging success, as that would loosen their stranglehold on Brazzaville."

"Could your connections at Occidental approach Bissoula? Cash for oil concessions, concessions that would only marginally impact ELF's, but still provide a sound return on a political investment?" Quinton asked. He looked at Schmidt, who knew what was coming, but was too late to ward off the question.

"That is not our business!" Fareid was standing now, and his eyes had grown large. "What Bissoula does with oil concessions does not concern us! This issue must not be mentioned again!"

Quinton looked at Schmidt, who was avoiding his gaze. *Something doesn't smell right*, Quinton thought, and plowed ahead. "If Oxy is able to pull this off, and we are none the wiser, then that helps QSCI on two fronts: one, Bissoula's government stays in office (and we get paid), and two, we are out of the firing line when ELF comes a-calling, and they will if Occidental waltzes onto the dance floor."

"Be that as it may," Fareid said, "just remember what Thomas Kanza said about what may come from mixing in the oil business, my friend: 'A bullet may find you!' A bullet or a knife or worse, although what could be worse, I am uncertain."

Schmidt interjected, "We have other opportunities, Daniel. Fareid is right. Let's capitalize on those and leave petroleum to the wolves."

"Left to the wolves it is," Quinton said. "Here's hoping some bridge loan, oil-generated or not, magically appears in Brazzaville so the honest and hard-working principals of QSCI are compensated for their modest efforts. Efforts to advance the cause of democracy in the Congo."

"Indeed. To confounding the wolves!" Schmidt toasted, without a glass.

"Yes," Fareid said, but he was looking out the window as if someone he would recognize might appear.

"Good afternoon, gentlemen. I am Inspector Morain from the *Police Nationale*," the detective said as he addressed the group in the quiet corner of the lobby, his hand on the back of Fareid's chair. "Monsieur Chamoun?" he asked bowing slightly toward Fareid. "The concierge at the Royal Monceau suggested I might find you here."

"I am Chamoun. How may I help you?" Fareid stood during the exchange, then motioned the Inspector to an empty chair.

"Yes, thank you," Morain said, then turned to the two Americans as Fareid introduced them: "Inspector, Dr. Lake Schmidt, and Cdr. Daniel Quinton, colleagues."

"Gentlemen." Morain then shifted his weight, and turned toward Fareid: "Are you acquainted with a man named Al-Hami Makel?" The Inspector stared straight into Fareid's eyes waiting for the lie, which he would identify unfailingly, or the truth, with which Fareid now obliged him.

"Yes, we are old friends," Fareid said. "What has happened? We were together yesterday, and all was well. Exceedingly well. We are to meet this evening." Fareid knew the answer would not be good.

"I must regretfully inform you that Monsieur Makel is dead. He has been murdered." Again Morain looked for a reaction, a response of any sort that might give him a line of questioning to follow.

Fareid clenched his jaw. "Where was he killed, and how?" He looked intently at Morain. "Has the body been positively indentified?"

Morain: "Makel was identified through his passport, and we are running his prints now, to confirm. You say he was a friend? You knew him for how long?" The Inspector watched Fareid respond, looking for a twitch, a change in skin tone, a widening of the irises in the big man's eyes, any subtle suggestion of deception.

"Since boarding school," Fareid said, looking at Morain straight on. "Al-Hami was from Alexandria, but lived in Cairo after he returned from school.

"He is . . . he was a respected attorney, and a decent human being." Fareid looked away from the policeman and managed to keep his rage in check by clenching his teeth, a reaction Morain noted. "Any apparent motive? Was it robbery? Did it appear personal?"

Morain stood and shook his head slowly. "Regrettably, Monsieur, I am unable to discuss all of the details of the investigation. I am curious, however, if you are familiar with a knife-like weapon that has Arabic inscribed on what appears to be a bone or ivory handle? The blade itself is long—24 centimeters or so—and narrow."

"Al-Hami was stabbed? He is a very cautious man; such an event seems very unlikely. Where did this happen?" Fareid now studied the Inspector.

"In a hair salon on Avenue Hoche. The other victim was the owner, a Scot known as Blue. Do you know the place or the man?"

Fareid shook his head. He looked vacantly across the lobby, trying to imagine the last scene of his friend's life. Morain continued, "He was having a shave, and his face was covered by a towel, it appeared. He would not have seen his attacker."

"What does the inscription on the handle say?" Fareid asked, returning his gaze to the Inspector. "The inscription in Arabic."

"Headquarters Group is having it translated. If you would take the time to examine the weapon, we could ask your help in translating the inscription. It may contain a colloquialism or idiomatic phrase, a meaning we might miss. But first, if you would be so kind as to identify the remains." Morain watched Fareid. "Your active assistance will have a positive effect on the tracking of your friend's killer, and the killer of the man we believe was an innocent bystander." The Inspector waited.

Fareid knew he was being read, and without a flicker of hesitation replied, "Whatever I might do to assist would be an honor. Neither Al-Hami Makel nor the other victim deserved to die in such a way. Are you sure the killer was not after the salon owner?"

Morain shook his head. "Makel was closest to the door. He died from a stab wound that pierced his heart; the blade went through the barber's sheet. We believe he was the first target, so we believe he was the intended victim. Monsieur Blue was farther away from the door, and by all appearances had time at least to make some defensive effort. Regrettably, it was unsuccessful."

He continued: "We received an emergency 'One Seven' call . . . equivalent to your 911 emergency service," Morain turned, acknowledging the Americans, "but we have been unable to coax the caller forward. We believe he saw the attack and may have some information about the killer, but for now," Morain shrugged, "we have very little."

"Except the murder weapon with Arabic on the handle," Fareid reminded him.

"*Oui, Monsieur.*" Morain bowed, and continued, "Pardon me for the intrusion, but we are moving ahead as quickly as possible with the investigation. Paris is a transient city, and when the players in the event are of different nationalities the likelihood the killer will flee the country is great. We believe a swift arrest will bring swift justice, *ne c'est pas?*"

The Inspector addressed Fareid directly: "Your assistance is most welcome, Monsieur Chamoun. I look forward to seeing you tomorrow morning at the Station. Should you think of anything relevant, or should you believe you are in imminent danger, please call me at anytime of the day or the night. I suggest you remain most vigilant."

Morain handed Chamoun his card and bowed to Schmidt and Quinton individually, then turned and left. He strode resolutely across the lobby and was quickly on the sidewalk, bright with the sunlight of early afternoon, hailing his driver.

CHAPTER
TWENTY-SEVEN

THE GEORGES V'S fourth floor hallway leading to the conference room, where those seeking restoration of Congolese government funds would meet was like a bad dream. *Even Fellini would have blushed at this scene of nightmarish excess*, Quinton thought. The rooms of the Congolese delegation lining the hall were littered with boxes of electronics, Louis Vuitton luggage, audio/visual games, bolts of embroidered fabric, and an assorted array of Western Civilization's retail detritus.

At the far end of the hallway, Michael Ndono waved the group forward, past the rooms of his compatriots and their families, and through the maze of acquisitions, to join him and the Foreign Minister in the conference room. Why the Americans seemed taken aback by the collection of booty was a puzzlement to Ndono. "Come this way, you are headed in the right direction," he called, smiling.

"If a goodly portion of those stolen monies aren't recovered, El Presidente will be wading in deep Kim Chee," Quinton said to

Schmidt, who was intent on stepping around a stack of boxed stereo components.

"Indeed. As you suggest with your mixed cultural metaphor, that is true. Very true."

A few paces behind the pair, Fareid had buttonholed Robert James, the Director of Kroll Associates, Paris, and was coaxing him along the passageway. "This is not out of the ordinary," Fareid said casually to James, hopeful the Director would not be put off by the unseemly extravagance of the Congolese entourage.

James: "Yes, I suppose so."

"There!" Fareid pointed toward the end of the gauntlet, "There is Ndono."

When the four men reached the small conference room, Ndono, who stood politely inside the double door, ushered them in. Maurice Gaomu, wearing a pair of wire-rimmed glasses, sat at the far side of a linen covered conference table behind an arrangement of water glasses, notepads and pens. His hands were folded serenely in front of him on the table.

"Your Excellency," Ndono began, "May I introduce Fareid Chamoun, his colleagues Dr. Lake Schmidt and Daniel Quinton, and from Kroll Associates, Mr. Robert James."

His Excellency, the Foreign Minister of the Republic of the Congo, Monsieur Maurice Gaomu, remained seated, but raised his hands upward and his palms outward in a welcoming gesture. "Gentlemen, thank you for joining me this evening. Please be seated." He motioned for the group to sit, making an effort to appear unconcerned, but keenly interested in how the politics of positioning at the table would sort itself out.

Fareid apologetically seated himself next to the Foreign Minister, saying, "In the event I am needed to translate." He motioned for James to sit next to him, and with a nod to the two Americans, indicated they might want to sit on the other side of Gaomu's assistant, Ndono.

Gaomu took note of the directed pecking order and addressed Fareid. "Mr. Ndono has explained our task, and we have been granted permission by the President's Office to pursue this theft of national assets." Gaomu continued, "I am a direct man, so I will tell you directly: the resolution of this issue is essential to the survival of this government. Will you be able to help?"

Robert James raised himself off his seat with his hands and adjusted his sitting position, turning to Fareid, then back to Gaomu, "Kroll Associates stands ready to serve your needs, Excellency."

"As do I and my associates," Fareid said, with a nod toward Quinton and Schmidt.

"Very well, gentlemen, let's begin." Gaomu consulted his notes, encased in a leather binder, and said to the group as he peered over his reading glasses, "Estimates from the Ministers of Oil and Finance place the monies stolen by former President Sassou-Nguesso at $800 million. Regrettably, they are not in a single container under a park bench on the Avenue Marshall Foch. We believe our treasury has been disbursed to such far flung locations as Hong Kong, Monaco, the Caribbean, Zurich, and here, especially here in Paris."

"My question to you," Gaomu paused and looked individually at each of those gathered at the table, "is this: What is our next step, should we agree to go forward?"

Fareid looked to his left at Robert James, who was waiting for his cue. James spoke, "Excellency, with the help of QSCI, Kroll Associates is ready to proceed on behalf of the Bissoula government once we have a formal written agreement. In that agreement, we will be looking for the following components: permission to act on the government's behalf in the recovery of state funds; full cooperation of the Ministers of Oil and Finance, or any other Department involved in the flow of oil revenues; and finally, a compensation agreement wherein QSCI receives an amount agreed upon by separate document, and Kroll Associates receives an initial retainer of $100,000 to begin preliminary investigation." James took a controlled breath, then continued, "We will establish an office in Brazzaville. Weekly progress reports will be provided to the government's representative concerning the identification, validation and recovery of the stolen assets, and with a senior Kroll associate to brief your designated representative on demand." James looked around the table with a confident air, picking up steam in his delivery, as he believed his presentation made perfect sense and held the promise of an enormous return flow of revenue which rightly belonged to the government of the Democratic Republic of the Congo.

"This appears a sound and valid project, one of mutual benefit, and one which Kroll and our friends at QSCI are anxious to get underway." James finished with a flourish and a gesture of inclusion, his arms raised in a motion of embrace.

Maurice Gaomu sat implacably, looking first at James, then at the rest of the group. Quinton, Schmidt and Chamoun nodded their support for James' fervent pitch for undertaking *Projet Monet*, but the $100,000 retainer for a government that teetered on the brink of collapse was clearly a deal-breaker for Gaomu. This was an untenable position. A minister could not recommend to his President the expenditure of money in the mere hopes of recovering stolen assets that were sequestered around the world. "Perhaps a contingency-based fee . . ."

Gaomu directed his question to James, but it was intended for Chamoun, Quinton and Schmidt as well. "I am authorized to go forward on a contingency basis, but not on a retainer. An agreement could be reached on compensation for all as recovered monies arrive in Brazzaville. This is certainly a fair arrangement. Will you agree to discussing this as a way to proceed?"

Quinton and Schmidt looked hopefully toward Fareid, who had turned toward Robert James. "Robert, this could be a once-in-a-career opportunity. You must prevail upon New York to allow you to operate in the framework suggested by the Foreign Minister."

James looked around the room and felt isolated. This was not, nor would it ever be in James' view, a policy that Jules Kroll would approve. Any employment contract must include a retainer. Particularly where nascent governments were involved, no matter how high minded.

"I will forward your proposal to New York so that we might further our talks. I must tell you, Excellency, the chances are remote that company policy will be altered for this project, or any project for that matter. The retainer principle is bedrock to Kroll's business model. I am unable to change that; I can only request a variance. But I tell you now, it is like praying for rain in the desert."

James rose to make his apologies, and bowed towards Gaomu. He glanced towards the others, but returned his attention to the Foreign Minister, saying, "If you are able to move on the retainer, we will press forward vigorously. Kroll believes in your democratization of the Congo."

Gaomu smiled, and said softly, "But not quite enough to be partners in recovering stolen funds without up front payment."

"We, at the end of the day, are just a business, Excellency," James said. He gathered up his satchel and papers, and walked slowly to the conference room doors. Turning just before he reached the exit, he said, "May you meet with the utmost success in your good and honest efforts."

And that, my friends, is a showstopper, Quinton thought. He looked across the table toward Schmidt, then Fareid. Schmidt returned his gaze with an expression of concern. Fareid was speaking quietly with the Foreign Minister.

Nodding and separating himself from Fareid, Gaomu said, "Thank you, gentlemen. Thank you for your work on our behalf." Gaomu stood then turned to Quinton, Schmidt, and finally Fareid. "We must not give up. My staff," he looked over at Michael Ndono, "will keep you informed of our progress. Please enjoy the rest of the evening. This is, after all, Paris." In spite of his up-note finish to the meeting, it was evident to those who remained in the room Gaomu was not going to enjoy the rest of his evening

Quinton and Schmidt headed for the doors, and Fareid motioned he would be with them in just one minute. He took the Foreign Minister gently by the arm and moved to the far side of the room. They stood briefly by the floor-to-ceiling windows, bathed in the exterior lighting that lit up the façade of the hotel, and exchanged a few words, after which Fareid bowed slightly, turned and headed to join his friends.

CHAPTER TWENTY-EIGHT

THE THIRD FLOOR hallway carpet of the Royal Monceau was Sarouk in design and seemed familiar to Fareid. *Yes, in one of my father's houses*, he thought. *Repeated patterns, even when complex, are recognizable when seen often enough.* Fareid reflected on the intricacy of the rose and pink silk pattern of the rug as he absentmindedly ran his fingers along the enameled chair rail that ran the length of the hall. He was on his way to his room after bidding good night to his partners, and his thoughts were filled with what he might say to President Bissoula. It was clear to him that *Projet Monet* was not going forward. *The pattern again,* he thought.

Inside the room, Fareid removed his suit coat and folded it neatly onto the bed. He pulled up the wingback chair next to the night table and picked up the telephone. "I would like to place a long distance call to Brazzaville, the Congo," he informed the hotel operator, providing the number to Pascal Bissoula's private residence. With his left hand he loosened his necktie, ran his fingers back across his forehead, then through his hair. The line hummed, but no voice was heard. Then:

"Monsieur Chamoun, I have President Bissoula on the line," Marie Badoun said.

"*Merci, Madame.*"

On the other end, Bissoula began, "Fareid. *Ça va, mon vieux.*"

"I am well, Your Excellency." Fareid said flatly.

"Ah," the President said. "Normally I am unable to read you by your voice, but I am afraid, judging your tone, the Kroll meeting went in a direction other than we hoped." Bissoula paused. When no response came, he said "Fareid?"

"Papa," Fareid answered quietly, "Kroll will not undertake the project without a retainer. And my private discussion with their Paris man leads me to believe that the recovery will take years to bear fruit."

"We do not have years, Fareid."

"This I know."

"Then," Bissoula said quietly, "it is time for the option we discussed earlier. Are you confident we can have a quick and successful result?"

"With your personal and official guarantee to the head of the entity concerned, there will be an irrevocable agreement to complete the transaction we discussed, yes. Absolutely yes," Fareid said. His mental list for activating the funding from Occidental Petroleum had begun at the conclusion of the meeting with Ngaomu. Now, the blocks were being checked off at an increasing pace.

"Good." Bissoula concluded by saying, "When you return to Brazzaville we will flesh out the details, but I want you to initiate the appropriate contact to start the program. This evening, if it is possible. We have very little time. Good night, Fareid."

"*Dorme bien*, Excellency." Fareid hung up the phone, then picked it up again. To the hotel operator: "London exchange, please," and provided the telephone number for the flat in Cadogan Square.

When Nawala answered, Fareid said, "Hello, my loyal friend. How are you keeping?"

"Oh! Mr. Chamoun. All is well. All is well. It is raining here, of course." Nawala fussed with her hair, as if Fareid could see her over the phone line.

"Of course," Fareid said. Then quickly: "I will be abroad a few more weeks, so I need you to water the plants in the foyer, especially the oleander."

"Of course, as soon as we hang up, Mr. Chamoun."

"Thank you, my habbibi. I will call you in a few days," and Fareid hung up.

Nawala sat looking at the phone and at her hand still on the receiver. It shook slightly, rattling the receiver softly in its cradle. *I much prefer cooking, even washing up,* she thought, and snatched her hand back into her lap. She rose and scurried into the foyer, where the silk oleander sat in a terra cotta planter. *I must knock the dust off the leaves,* she thought, *after I am finished.* The envelope was hidden under the moss at the base of the plant, and she picked it up quickly, looking nervously at the front door.

In the kitchen, Nawala opened the letter, read its brief contents, and collapsed the paper together in her hands; then she re-opened it and read the contents again. She ripped the letter into small pieces, and stuffed the remains into what was left of an eggplant that had been scraped out for her evening meal of babbaganoush, kibbe and tabouli. Nawala shoved the purple vegetable containing Fareid's instructions deep into the trash, wiped her hands on her apron, and went to get her raincoat.

On the northeast corner of Cadogan Square, the light in the red phone booth glowed dimly. *I pray it has not been vandalized*, Nawala thought, as she scuttled across the street, raincoat draped above her head. Inside the booth, she shook off the rain and dialed the operator.

"Dallas, Texas. Occidental Petroleum," and provided the number. Then, to the voice that answered, Nawala asked: "Is this the office on the 13th floor?"

"We have no 13th floor."

Nawala squinted, and focused all her efforts to stay on track. "Then this is what I must say: 'Proceed with all haste. Pre-conditions agreed. Equestrian sends'." Nawala squeezed her eyes tightly, hoping she had transmitted the message correctly.

"Thank you, and good night." The line went dead.

The beleaguered woman slumped against the inside of the phone booth, staring at the flat across the square through the rain-splattered glass. She stayed there for minutes that passed uncounted. When Nawala finally opened the door to return to the flat the rain had stopped, but low clouds scudded across the tops of the buildings surrounding the square. She looked up and down the dimly lit street and, seeing no one, gathered herself up for another dash across the puddles that glistened now in what small light shone from the streetlamps.

The watcher on the far side of the park took a last pull on his cigarette and dropped it at his feet. The butt end hit the damp ground, hissed and was quickly extinguished. He had never taken his eyes off the woman now entering the street level entrance to the Cadogan Square flat. Waiting for the woman to close the heavy door opening to the flight of stairs, the man moved steadily toward the phone booth and once inside, left the door partially opened to keep the light from coming on. He picked up the receiver and placed a call. As he waited for an answer from the other end of the line, the lights in the living room of the second floor flat across the street were turned out, one by one.

CHAPTER TWENTY-NINE

THE FRESH FLOWER kiosk carried a load that was in full bloom. Early morning passersby not yet inclined to buy a token of affection, or a gesture that would win forgiveness, scurried or drudged by, postures dependent on their prospects for the day. The old woman vendor, whom locals swore had been there since the Armistice, fussed with her wares and made a pass at fluffing the threadlike wisps of her remaining hair. Her smile was infectious, in spite of being virtually toothless.

Even though the morning was starting slowly, she remained upbeat. Gilles Simonet, the Prefect of Police, invariably bought a boutonnière for his suit jacket from the sidewalk florist, and the first transaction of the day was in the books. Simonet would step from his driven sedan, purchase his flower, and stroll toward the Place Louis Lapine, where the Prefecture and Headquarters of the Paris Police overlooked Rue de Letuce.

The Prefect's destination was an imposing building located in the Île de la Cité, and scattered within were the various offices of the Central

Directorate of Judicial Police. From the upper reaches of the northeast parapet, Simonet's office commanded a view of the gothic towers and flying buttresses of the Cathedral of Notre Dame, two blocks to the southeast. "At last, I rise above the Church," he would note, as he looked out across the Hopitaux-Publique de Paris and down at the famed Cathedral.

Today Simonet was leaning forward, walking at a determined pace. He almost brushed by the flower vendor without his usual exchange, but the resolute purveyor held out a small sample, and said, "Monsieur Simonet?"

"Of course," he said, reaching for a franc note, "My apologies. My mind was elsewhere."

The murders of the Egyptian lawyer and the salon owner had become particularly bothersome to Simonet, as the Minister of Justice was riding him hard for a successful conclusion to his investigation. The case had been sensationalized in *Le Monde*, and had a rabid following among the 'ghoul keepers,' as Simonet called the homicide followers. Toward fending off the irksome Minister, the Prefect had scheduled daily briefings from the Inspector Divisionaire and his principal investigator, Inspector Morain.

This morning, the two detectives were on their way to his office from the Homicide Division, referred to only by its address "36 Quai des Orfévres." Simonet was not happy with the progress to date. *We should have brought this bastarde to ground already*, he thought. *Witnesses, forensic evidence, this Arabic pig sticker . . . What is the delay!? . . .*

He rehearsed his rant while marching across the open courtyard, affixing the floret into his buttonhole. *And you will find a motive to pull this together, Morain!* Simonet gave his lapel a tug and a flick with manicured fingers and opened the door to his private entry, satisfied with both his look and his resolve to bring the messiness to a close.

"Monsieur? You are a distinguished and handsome man, *c'est vrai.* You must have a fair one who needs and deserves a fresh flower!" Up came the floral offering, followed by a toothless smile.

The man held up his index finger and moved it side to side. Smiling, he said, "Not at the moment, my little habbibi, but perhaps after the finish of business." Fareid straightened his tie, and continued his advance toward the meeting with Morain.

I will find the piece of crumpled dung that did this to you, Al-Hami, and kill him. This I swear. He made a fist with his right hand, brought it to his face and kissed the back of his thumb. Fareid's eyes were closed, and his jaws clenched.

Inspector Morain sat in a metal chair at a plain table in a windowless space, a setting that could have been any of a hundred interrogation rooms the world over. Two CCTV cameras were tucked in the upper corners, between the gray ceiling and the even grayer walls. A uniformed Corporal stood outside, and could be seen through the wire reinforced glass panel in the upper half of the door.

Morain toyed with a plastic bag that contained the murder weapon used to kill the Egyptian lawyer, Al-hami Makel. Dark, crusted blood stains remained on the blade. He could make out the Arabic script on the knife handle, but it appeared to him as decorative scroll and nothing more. The linguists at Headquarters had made a rough translation, but were uncertain about its accuracy. "Middle Arabic, probably Egyptian, but not sure how it translates in the broad sense," the chief translator had advised Morain. "The dagger is old, but the inscription appears recent," he added.

Let's see how our Lebanese friend Chamoun reads it, he thought. Movement at the interrogation room door caught Morain's eye, and Fareid entered the room, ushered in by the Corporal.

"Monsieur Chamoun," Morain said, standing. The metal chair scraped on the floor.

"Inspector," Fareid said, his eyes already on the bagged evidence.

Morain followed his glance, then pointed to the dagger: "Here is the weapon, but first let me express my gratitude for your identifying the remains of your friend . . ."

"Al-Hami Makel," Fareid finished for him. "Anything I can do to assist." His eyes returned to the knife.

"Please," Morain motioned for Fareid to sit. "Allow me." Morain sat opposite and carefully opened the plastic bag, gingerly extracting the weapon with thumb and forefinger. "Here," he pointed, "Here is the Arabic inscription. Our linguists have translated, but feel there is a nuance they are missing. What do you think?" He handed Fareid the knife, adding, "Please, gently."

Fareid took the knife and held it by the handle, rolling the ivory slightly to see the carefully carved message. A flicker of recognition flashed over his eyes, then was gone. Morain thought he saw the glint, but was not certain.

"Monsieur," Morain asked, "how do you read this? What does it say? Perhaps more importantly, what does it mean?"

"It says: '*El Faredeesh. Ragham Quz'ah allah anfu.*' It is Egyptian Arabic, and I believe it translates: 'The Horseman. May the Dwarf and God rub his nose in the sand.' It is an old curse, but I do not know its significance," Fareid said, locking eyes with the Inspector.

That 'Quz'ah' could also be translated as ELF need not be mentioned, Fareid thought. He fought to remain unemotional and unreadable. He finished his thought: *Laurent Ballieux, you had best find a place where God has lost his shoe, and stay there. Otherwise I will find you. Then I will kill you.*

"No other meaning?" Morain asked, again looking for the slightest indication of deception.

"None of which I am aware."

Holding it with all the caution he had been advised, Fareid returned the knife. He stood and bowed slightly toward the Inspector, saying, "I trust you will prosecute this investigation with all your skill and determination. If I might assist further, please call me. I believe you have my card, by way of my late friend, Monsieur Makel."

Morain stood, but paused for one more look. "Yes, of course, Monsieur Chamoun." Holding Fareid's gaze, Morain said, "You are free to go. Please enjoy the rest of the day."

"And you, Inspector."

"Oh, and one more thing, Monsieur. Please leave your Brazzaville address with my Corporal. *Bon voyage.*"

When the door closed, and Morain was alone in the room, he looked at the knife on the table and said, "There was more to it. Of that I am sure."

CHAPTER THIRTY

THE FLIGHT FROM Paris to Brazzaville was quiet. Quinton and Schmidt sat several seats apart, as the flight was barely half occupied. Fareid sat aft in the smoking section, where there were few empty seats and the haze of tobacco smoke was thick and eyewatering.

Schmidt occasionally wandered back to the restroom, and he and Fareid would nod at one another. Neither felt compelled to discuss the events of recent days. The all-but-evaporated prospect of the implementation of *Projet Monet* had been deflating for Quinton and Schmidt, but Fareid remained, as usual, relaxed and unreadable.

"This is just one project, my professor," Fareid had said to buoy the flagging spirits of both men. Quinton and Schmidt had agreed.

"I'll have to return all that furniture for the villa in the South of France I had moved into in my mind," Schmidt said. "*Quelle dommage.*"

"Suppose my 52' Hatteras in the Keys goes back on the market. Can't remember if I saw myself in the yellow or dark blue hull." Quinton squinted as if staring down the wake from the Sportfisherman's flybridge. *Fish not on,* he thought.

Fareid: "Back to Brazzaville, then."

The breeze off the Congo River fanned the palm fronds around the hotel's pool corner cabana, and Steve Farber and Carey Price found the afternoon exceedingly fine.

"'The golden afternoon came down as slowly as age to a happy man'," Farber quoted, looking around him and at the tops of the trees swaying rhythmically in the sun.

"Well said," Price noted, also enjoying the moment. "Yours?"

"No, Steinbeck's actually. But thanks for the thought." Farber slowly scanned the pool area, then looked up at the hotel towering over the river. He shielded his eyes from the blue brightness of the African sky. "Have you seen Mark today?"

Price: "Not since breakfast yesterday. Missed him at dinner. Seems to be spending most of his time in the library and in the garden."

"May I get you another drink?" the flight attendant asked Laurent Ballieux. While inquiring, she kept her distance from the foul-smelling, unshaven passenger, thinking, *If I bring him one or two more drinks, perhaps the cretin will pass out and the trip to Brazzaville will pass much more pleasantly.* She had miscalculated.

"Why don't you bring me two, and save your pretty little ass an extra trip?" Ballieux breathed. The air around his seat became sodden with dank vapor.

The flight attendant recoiled in revulsion, but reflexively said, "Right away, Monsieur."

Ballieux lit up another cigarette and looked out the window at black nothingness. He could see his reflection in the plexiglass, but used the opportunity to scan the other passengers without facing them directly. *Had I taken the earlier flight with Fareid, I could have killed him in the airplane,* he thought. *Instead I'm stuck with a planeload of fat noires and ugly Germans. God, how I hate them all.*

"Your drinks, Monsieur." The flight attendant wrested her arm free from the clutching grasp of the brooding man, who then took the whiskies and set them on the seatback table.

"Sow," he grunted as the attendant moved quickly down the aisle toward the galley.

In the terminal lobby at the Aeroport Maya Maya in Brazzaville, arriving and departing passengers milled about, dragged enormous bags across the concrete floor, and loaded up on duty free stock. Others waited in line to use the public telephones.

At the phone kiosk closest to the terminal's front windows, Laurent Ballieux elbowed his way past a colorfully dressed older woman, who offered only a mild protest. "I will give up my place. I do *not* want to be near that man," she said quietly to herself, taking a step back. "No, my goodness, no."

Ballieux picked up the telephone and guarded the receiver with his left hand. In a low growl, he directed the operator to place a call. The line was connected. "Monsieur Liberte?" Ballieux asked.

"*Oui,*" Georges Danou responded.

"I am here. The business is only partially finished, and . . . ."

"When?" Danou interrupted.

"The week will not end without the pestilence being eradicated," Ballieux said, not sure he used the right phrase to describe murdering Fareid, but it felt good to say it.

The line at the other went dead. Ballieux hung up, looked at the receiver and then spat on it. He walked off toward the terminal entrance, leaving the phone dangling by its cord. The line of people waiting to follow him at the kiosk quickly dissolved. Some looked for another phone, and some, like the colorfully dressed woman, wondered whether making a phone call was really that necessary.

CHAPTER THIRTY-ONE

MORNING CAME TO the banks of the Congo river as it did most days of the year: sun ascending in a clear sky, wind barely perceptible, just enough to ruffle the tops of thin black plumes of smoke rising from wood fires in villages along the river bank. In the distance, towering cumulus held the promise of afternoon rain.

Around the M'Bamou Palace Hotel pool deck area, staff in starched white coats bustled about, setting up long tables for the breakfast buffet. The men snapped white linen table clothes with flare, draping the coverings across tables with agility and grace to impress the young girls folding napkins not far away. The girls, uniformed in bright floral outfits, pretended not to watch the exaggerated performance. The performers pretended not to care.

By the time the American Delegation gathered in the cabanas near the pool, the array of flowers and breakfast wonders were flawlessly arranged. The bamboo-and-palm-frond bar next to the buffet was open. The bartender sliced limes and stalks of celery, preparing for the Bloody Marys that would soon line the bar top. The drinks would disappear into the groping hands of thirsty hotel guests, like bait fish under a swirl of gannets.

"Sorry to hear the Paris trip wasn't the resounding success you thought it might be," Price said to Quinton and Schmidt. The others nodded an agreement.

"S'pose it could have been a little better, but 'Softly, softly catchee monkey' as they say." Schmidt grinned. "We're not discouraged. 'The river flows slowly' and 'Rome wasn't built in a day' . . ."

"And 'the great, green, greasy Limpopo River is all set about with fever trees,'" Quinton added, staring off into the distance.

Farber looked at Price, and they both looked quizzically at Quinton.

Schmidt said, "Thank you, Daniel."

"Wonder what Molly Bowen is wearing today. She'd just be getting ready to go to work at Emily's," Quinton muttered, impervious to the odd looks from his colleagues.

"Uncertain to know from this distance," answered Farber. "But this I do know—regardless of distance—there are no finer bare shoulders or décolletage in all of Beaufort County."

Quinton snapped back into the present. "Yes. Exactly what you said." He paused, then added, "What did you say?"

"Just recalling some of Molly's more attention-grabbing attributes. Ones she seems to exhibit with a little added flair when you're among the patrons, Daniel." Farber added, "Trust that hasn't escaped your notice."

"Has not." Quinton's gaze returned to the far treetops across the river.

Fareid appeared, emerging from the hotel lobby wearing a blue silk shirt and cream slacks. He waved and smiled when he saw the group, and headed for their cabana. "Where is Mr. Adrian?" he asked, pulling up a wicker chair.

"Said he would be joining us for the second round of tomato drinks," Steve Farber said. "Welcome back to Brazzaville, Fareid." Farber touched his wire-rimmed glasses and leaned forward. "Very sad and distressing to hear about the murder of your friend, Mr. Makel."

Fareid glanced quickly at Quinton and Schmidt, and then said, "It is very sad, yes." Lowering his voice, he looked at each of the men. "As I said some weeks ago, my fear was that our efforts would be hindered by banana skins in our path, or worse. Plainly, 'worse' has happened.

"I believe the man who killed the woman in the market and murdered my friend Al-Hami is responsible for hampering our efforts to help the government of the Congo. He is one and the same person." Fareid paused and, begging forgiveness of the group, lit up a cigarette.

"His name is Laurent Ballieux, and he is tracking our group wherever we go." He exhaled a stream of smoke upward over the heads of the men, before continuing. "I believe Ballieux has a collaborator," Fareid looked at the group, "and I fear we are at risk."

The others looked around the group, and Farber offered, "Mark has been spending time with Dr. Nguomo. You don't imagine . . ."

Fareid said, "Spending time?" The cigarette in his right hand was abruptly suspended in mid-journey.

"Well, yes. He ran into Nguomo at the hotel library, and I believe they had lunch one day in the garden. But after all, Nguomo treated Mark for his affliction and he recovered quickly!" Farber said.

Fareid was leaning forward in his chair, arms on the table, and was about to speak when Price said, "Look, here comes Mark."

The group turned toward the lobby, and Mark Adrian, sporting an African dashiki draped loosely over a pair of old jeans and bare feet stuck in leather toe-ring flip-flops, ambled across the pool deck toward the cabana. He waved good-naturedly.

"Great Ramar of the Jungle, he's gone native," Quinton said quietly.

Adrian greeted each of the men, and the group gathered closer around the table as he sat down to join them Fareid studied the brightly clad man talking with his friends. Adrian waved to the waiter, pointed to one of the breakfast cocktails, and made a circular motion with his forefinger, calling for another round. No one protested.

The quick movement nearby of a man in a dark jacket caught Fareid's eye first. Exploding out of his chair, the big Lebanese stopped and drew off his jacket, wrapping it around his left arm like a lion tamer.

The dark-jacketed man was running now, not toward the Americans, but at an angle to intercept another man who was aggressively closing on the group just yards away, eyes fixed intently on Fareid Chamoun.

"DuLang!" Adrian shouted at the dark-jacketed man. He leapt from his seat, running toward the intersection where DuLang and the attacker would collide. Adrian was only a stride or two ahead of Fareid.

"Fulbert! No!" Adrian was now in full sprint. "Not what we planned! My job, goddammit, that's my job!" His voice was raspy and came in short bursts.

The thick and disheveled man with his eyes on Fareid reached into his coat pocket, struggling to extract a weapon. He continued his advance, with only a sideward glance toward DuLang, who had picked up a full head of steam.

"Ballieux!" Dulang screamed.

Fareid stopped, then whirled to shout to his friends, "Everybody down!" This allowed DuLang and Adrian to continue on their collision course moving closer to Ballieux.

With the group at the tables now scattered on the floor, Fareid turned back to charge Laurent Ballieux. The man had stopped and drawn a

9mm Beretta. He stood in a tactical firing position: legs spread apart, two hands gripping the handgun.

DuLang, Adrian, and Ballieux all converged as Ballieux was raising his handgun to shoot Fareid. From his jacket pocket, DuLang had pulled a gold and black fountain pen, raised it over his head and started a downward thrust.

Ballieux saw Dulang raising his arm and turned his attention away from Fareid to confront the enraged man. Adrian, a split second behind Dulang's plunge, caught the hand holding the fountain pen syringe at the wrist and deflected the blow. The struggling pair fell with their full weight into Ballieux, knocking his weapon downward. A chambered round from the Beretta discharged as they tumbled, exploding into the ELF agent's leg.

Ballieux screamed as blood spurted from the torn limb, his trousers quickly soaked by the wound. As Adrian and DuLang continued to battle, the American tripped backwards over the fallen Ballieux and DuLang fell forward, Adrian's hand still grasping and pulling his wrist.

Both men were locked together wrestling over the fountain pen when a violent downward thrust by the pair plunged the nib deep into the rib cage of the fallen Ballieux. His eyes bulged in fear and surprise, and he gasped and shuddered, fighting for breath. The two men rolled off the wounded assassin.

Fareid was on Ballieux before the man could move, and kicked the Beretta away. He grabbed Ballieux by the throat, and pulled his face to within inches while he squeezed.

"Fareid! No!" Quinton was pulling the big man off of Ballieux, Schmidt not far behind calling for help from the hotel staff.

A man in a tan suit came running from the lobby toward the fracas in response to the cries of alarm from the Americans.

CHAPTER THIRTY-TWO

WHEN INSPECTOR MORAIN arrived in Brazzaville, he had ordered a taxi to the M'Bamou Palace and paid the driver 100 CFAs to make it to the riverside hotel in record time. He contemplated flashing his National Police badge and documents from the Palais de Justice, but knew a wad of bills would hold more sway.

"Another 100 if you make it without stopping, and without hitting anyone."

The white Mercedes diesel belched black smoke as the driver downshifted and blew his horn at the annoying traffic impeding his bonus. "Yes, but of course!"

Morain had learned of Fareids's departure only after the airliner had lifted off, so he was too late to make the same flight. *The man who killed in Paris will follow the Lebanese, Chamoun,* he thought. They cannot know I have come to Brazzaville, neither Chamoun nor the butcher," he said quietly. "But I must move fast!"

"Monsieur?" The driver focused on his swerving efforts on the boulevard, had peeked in the rear view mirror in response.

"Nothing. Eyes on the road, *s'il vous plaît.*"

The taxi slid to halt in front of the lobby, and the driver bolted from the front seat to hold the door open for the detective. Examining his watch, he proudly announced, "From the airport, Monsieur, this is a new record."

Morain handed the man another wad of notes, grabbed his valise, and hurriedly put on his tan suit coat. He headed for the lobby without waiting, brushing by the valets and concierge. The commotion poolside, in view through the glass windows on the far side of the lobby, drove him into full sprint. Dropping his luggage on the marble floor, Morain bowled through a small group of astonished guests.

By the time Morain had reached the combatants in the cabana area, Ballieux was on the ground. Adrian sat holding his knees, DuLang next to him, both breathing hard, exhausted.

Fareid stood over Ballieux, and the Americans gathered around him.

"What has happened here?" Morain asked, looking at Fareid.

"This man," Fareid pointed with his jaw at the writhing Ballieux, "tried to shoot me, and," motioning to the rest of the group, "all of us." He continued, "But for the efforts of these two men, he would have succeeded. They knocked his hand down, and he shot himself."

"Do you know this man?" Morain asked, staring at Ballieux's bleeding leg wound.

"Not well. I saw him in Paris, and he seemed intent on creating havoc with my friends and colleagues. I don't know this, but I strongly suspect you will find his blood sample will match that found at the murder scene in the Avenue Hoche salon. He was not a victim there. This I also believe you will learn."

"And you know this . . ." Morain left the question hanging.

"I know this because you are an investigator with exceptional gifts, and I believe I tell you nothing you don't already suspect. I don't know these things to be fact, I merely believe you will learn them to be true," Fareid said.

While Morain was speaking with Fareid, Dulang had crawled over to Ballieux and whispered to the gasping man: "Marley Kinto."

"What?" Ballieux tried to reach DuLang's arm, but fell back, bewildered.

"Adrienne and Moko." Du Lang added.

"What are you saying, you filth?" Ballieux rasped.

"Marley Kinto. The name of the woman you killed in the market. And the little girl and her dog, the dog you shot: Adrienne and Moko." Dulang stared down at the man who had just been injected with the highly toxic protein ricin. In most adults the dose, $1/228^{th}$ the amount of an aspirin, would kill in a few hours. Dulang hoped it would take longer.

Morain turned to see DuLang gather himself up and rise to his feet, the detective again staring at the wound of the man on the ground. As Dulang stepped back, Morain approached the Congolese. He could see bloodstains from Ballieux's leg wound on the man's trousers, and a Mont Blanc fountain pen held loosely in his fingers.

"*Merci, Monsieur.* I will need this," Morain said, and gently took the pen from DuLang's limp hand. He looked at DuLang's face carefully, and saw an emotionless, empty landscape. Morain couldn't make out where the man was looking; for all he could tell DuLang was staring inside at the back of his own head.

While Morain and DuLang were facing one another, Fareid knelt down to look Ballieux in the face. Ballieux tried to muster enough saliva to spit at Fareid, but his lungs were drying and collapsing at a shocking rate.

"And my friend? My friend you killed? His name was Al-Hami Makel. And this is my face," he moved closer. "Something to think about as your miserable life ends." Ballieux twisted and turned in agony, then rested, his eyelids fluttering, eyeballs rolled back in his sockets. His arms and legs twitched then settled at angles that formed a human swastika.

Morain placed his hand under Fareid's arm and gently raised him up. Then, standing over Ballieux, he said "We need to get this man in hospital. His wound is serious, probably fatal."

The detective motioned for the ambulance attendants scurrying across the deck from the lobby to hurry up. To the hotel staff, who stood gawking at the scene: "Call the Robbery-Homicide Division, and make sure the handgun remains where it lies. Everything else, clean up. Everything." He looked at DuLang and Adrian and walked off beside the gurney as the attendants wheeled Ballieux away.

Morain ensured the cap on the fountain pen was tightly secured, then in a single fluid motion palmed the pen, dropped it in his pocket, and brought his hand up to slide back his coat sleeve to look at his watch. Even if someone were watching the detective closely, all that would have been noticed was a police official noting the time.

Morain surveyed the pool area, the windows of the rooms overlooking the cabana, and the lobby entrance. Nothing struck him as out of place. He turned toward the hotel and disappeared through the glass doors.

CHAPTER
THIRTY-THREE

THE AIR AFRIQUE jetliner had landed two hours ago in Brazzaville, and now sat in the hot sun on the tarmac awaiting the turnaround crew. The big turbo-fan jet engines still smelled hot from heat expansion, and the turbine blades inside the front of the gaping nacelles spun slowly, clattering in the wind blowing from the southwest. The white metal staircases had been rolled across the ramp and affixed to the forward and aft passenger doors, and the ground crew had attached large yellow tubing for the ground air blowers. With the main cabin readied, the Captain and First Officer had finally arrived, casually climbing the white AirStairs, turning toward the cockpit once aboard. The First Officer grabbed a cup of coffee and the flight planning paperwork. The Captain made the same remark to the brunette purser he had made every leg of every trip for twenty-eight years. The senior flight attendant laughed dutifully, and rolled her eyes after he passed.

Quinton and Schmidt stood on the ramp, talking quietly. Fareid had just left the airport after embracing each member of the delegation and bidding them safe travels. "We will meet in New York in a matter of weeks," he had told Quinton and Schmidt.

Steve Farber and Carey Price talked excitedly—Price about returning to Beaufort; Farber about returning to Beaufort so he could plan his next trip to Africa.

The steno pad in which Farber was scribbling was his fourth of the trip. It was nearly full. He made a few more strokes, then joined Quinton a few paces away. "Plans are to have dinner at your favorite restaurant when we arrive home. Any messages for your friend?" Farber then added, "Not sure this is apropos of anything, but Molly has a Fine Arts degree, reads Vonnegut and Brautigan, and likes to fly fish. Did you know that?"

"Did not, but thanks . . . even if you just made that up." Quinton said, smiling.

CHAPTER THIRTY-FOUR

MARK ADRIAN STOOD with the group, scanning the terminal in hopes Fulbert DuLang might have made it to see him off. Once, Adrian caught a flash of a brightly colored robe, and a green and yellow and red woven skull hat. The figure had turned toward him, a stranger, and then turned back and was gone, disappearing into the crowd like river fog that lifted and dissipated, melting into the trees.

Adrian and DuLang had become so profoundly linked while planning the downfall of Ballieux, the two had found themselves using the same phrases, ordering the same food, and drinking the same local beer. Before the plotting began, neither had been beer drinkers. Adrian had once referred to DuLang as his "other self," and DuLang had laughed at the impossibility of the idea. "Look at you, then look at me, my friend," he had said. Adrian had only blinked in reply. It made perfect sense to him.

The American found himself struggling to recall Dulang's features. They would come into focus, and then recede. Even what Adrian thought would leave an indelible imprint in his mind, the slashing, violent moments of the killing, the contortion of the dying man's face, were becoming gauzy and faded.

Amidst his blur and haziness, it occurred to him that while looking for DuLang he had been searching for his own image among the sea of eager faces inside the terminal. Had a man wearing a baseball cap, flowered shirt, and tortoise shell glasses appeared, he would have hailed him as his friend Dulang. Yet neither man surfaced from the swarm of travelers and officials; not Dulang, not Adrian, not even a shadow that might be mistaken for either of them.

The Congolese DuLang was now adrift, Adrian knew. He would be a lifelong fugitive from ELF, a vagabond in West Africa at best, with not the remotest hope of a quiet evening with anyone who cared about him, or what had happened. He would forever be too proud, and too fearful, to explain.

Adrian didn't give up looking for the man, his friend, and continued watching until the aircraft taxied away from the gate.

Fulbert Dulang had been questioned briefly by the Inspector, but released. Ballieux died later that afternoon.

The Coroner's Report read *A self-inflicted gunshot wound causing major trauma, coupled with as yet to be determined complications which accelerated the victim's exsanguination.*

CHAPTER THIRTY-FIVE

INSPECTOR MORAIN HAD packed for just a few days, so was able to carry his luggage on the return flight to Paris. He stuffed his valise in the overhead compartment and shoved his attaché case under the seat. Settling into his window seat, he reached into his coat pocket and withdrew a black and gold fountain pen.

The Mont Blanc Meisterstuck still smelled of the denatured alcohol in which it had been soaking for several hours in Morain's hotel room. He drew out his handkerchief, wiped it down for the third or fourth time, and rolled the pen between his thumb and forefinger like a cigar. After a moment, he carefully placed it in a *Police National* envelope. The Inspector looked out briefly over the receding African plains below, then pulled down the sunscreen. *I will complete my report when back in Paris, and perhaps send this to the evidence room,* he thought. With Ballieux's blood sample procured from the Brazzaville morgue, the knife with the Arabic inscription, and the physical evidence from the salon implicating the Belgian, Morain was satisfied Headquarters Group would consider the case closed. This result would be good enough for now.

The sound of the large mahogany door closing startled Fareid. He had just hung up the telephone on the desk of Mme. Badoun, and was surprised to see the President's secretary back in her office. Fareid had been told she would be out for an hour or so. The President was traveling abroad, and the anteroom to his office would be at Fareid's disposal, she had said.

Just prior to Madame's return, Fareid had been speaking with London. "She made the telephone call as instructed," the Cadogan Square watcher had advised Fareid. "The monies for the oil lease commitments have been wired, and the guaranteeing documents have been received on the other end."

"Very well, my friend," Fareid said, and hung up.

Marie Badoun smiled at Fareid and walked to her desk with the strut of a *de facto* head of state. By all measures, she outranked even the most senior of Ministers in Bissoula's absence. According to existing laws and regulations, nothing of governmental significance could occur during the absence of the Head of State, but Bissoula traveled more easily knowing that Badoun would enforce that principle.

"For you, Monsieur Chamoun," she said, handing Fareid a sealed envelope. "His Excellency asked that I make sure you received this before the day ended." Fareid nodded, and went to place the envelope in his jacket pocket.

"His Excellency also asked me to ensure that you read it right away," Badoun said.

"*Certainment.* As he wishes."

Fareid sliced open the envelope, pulled out the thick vellum paper, and translated to himself:

"*Monsieur Fareid Chamoun,*

The government and the people of the Democratic Republic of the Congo are in your debt. Your services to our country have been invaluable, and will help carry us forward into the company of the enlightened nations who embrace freedom, and by so doing, enjoy the benefit of free markets. With unending gratitude, I am, with very best personal regards,

Pascal Bissoula
President
Democratic Republic of the Congo

Mme. Badoun waited for Fareid to absorb the note. She moved around her desk to stand closer to him, and said softly, "Of course, Fareid, His Excellency will compensate you with more than this ceremonial token."

"I am confident he will, Madame. I have faith in the President."

"And you can rely on the man who will oversee the payments from Occidental," she added. As if on cue, the door from the President's office squeaked open and a short European man with a thick neck and longish arms stepped into the room. "Fareid, may I introduce the Special Master of the new oil lease funds, Georges Danou. He will be the intermediary for all financial transactions."

Fareid stared at the man, who moved forward offering his hand.

"He can be trusted," Mme. Badoun said.

CHAPTER THIRTY-SIX

FULBERT DULANG MADE his way back to Avenue de Amilcar Cabral, and found himself standing outside the front fence of the cinder block house. He looked up and down the dusty street and saw no one. At this time, on this day, no children played in the street. The equatorial sun beat down relentlessly, and DuLang considered that perhaps his black jacket was not a good choice for late afternoon on a hot day.

Removing the dark coat, he walked a few yards down the fence line to a patch of shade underneath a lone mango tree. Inexplicably, the leafy green boughs and the fruit and seeds of the tree were able to survive both the searing heat and lack of care.

When he reached the welcoming shadow, he folded his coat carefully and placed it in the middle of the shady spot. Seated beneath the tree, DuLang rubbed his forehead slowly with his fingertips and looked up through the branches toward the arc of the sun. Then he surveyed the boundaries of the shade outlined in the dust, calculating how long he could sit where he was before he would have to move.

The End

CPSIA information can be obtained at www.ICGtesting.com
Printed in the USA
LVOW132328270812

296184LV00003B/1/P